Billionaire Professors (The Geek Twins)

Julie L. Spencer

Click or scan here to request a complimentary book when you join my newsletter.

Copyright © 2021 by Julie L. Spencer

All rights reserved.

ISBN: 978-1-954666-01-6

www.AuthorJulieSpencer.com

Contents

Part One: Treasure Hunt

Dr. Nicholas Stephenson, PhD, Environmental Archaeology

A s told by Dr. Nicholas Stephenson, son of Frederick Stephenson, grandson of Alexandria (Cohen) Stephenson, great-grandson of Nicholas Cohen, great-great-grandson of Levi Cohen. Ten years after the passing of King Sayid, as the story begins...

Chapter One

The Geek Twins

"Dr. Stephenson, are you almost ready to go?" Nicholas called up the stairs to his twin brother, Levi. He already had the kickstand lifted, his helmet on, and his backpack strapped in place. His patience was wearing thin. "I have a meeting with a grad student in twenty minutes."

"Dr. Stephenson, why do you insist on calling me Dr. Stephenson when we're still at home?" Levi answered as he hurried downstairs to his mountain bike propped against the wall in their townhouse's ground floor garage. As Levi walked past the candy-apple-red Lamborghini Urus that they supposedly shared, Nicholas snapped at his brother.

"Don't scratch my car, dude." Nicholas realized a luxury SUV imported from Italy was the least likely choice of a Harvard professor, but he just couldn't resist temptation when he saw the concept car at the Beijing Auto Show. Without blinking an eye, he paid the $270,000 in advance and secured one of the coveted first runs of a thousand off the production line. The perks of growing up a billionaire.

"Did I, or did I not, pay for half of that beauty?" Levi asked, strapping on his bicycle helmet and lifting his bike from where it rested against the inside wall of the garage. "Not that I've ever driven it."

"I'm oldest. I get to drive." *When we drive*, Nicholas thought, rolling his bicycle out into the parking lot.

"By seven minutes. That hardly counts." Levi mounted his bike and reached for the button to close the garage door.

Nicholas watched longingly as his prized possession disappeared behind the protective barrier between his baby and the elements that threatened its paint job. He wondered if he'd ever get tired of looking at his new toy.

He shook off the nostalgia and pushed away from the curb, engaging the pedals of his bicycle.

The air was unseasonably warm for early November, and they were taking advantage of what could be their last day of riding their bicycles to work. They wouldn't have many more nice days like this. He let gravity and momentum pull him toward campus where they both taught.

As a professor of environmental archaeology, he worked closely with his brother's expertise in ancient languages to reconstruct past civilizations, particularly the Maya culture. Levi was at least partially fluent in all the main branches of the Mayan languages, particularly the Yucatec.

The Geek Twins, as their childhood friends used to call them, had been fascinated with the cultures in Guatemala all their adult lives. There were interwoven ties between their older brother, who served in an Army Special Forces unit during a humanitarian crisis along the Belize-Guatemala border, and their cousin who married a Guatemalan girl who was also somehow a distant cousin of theirs.

The confusing blood lines and generational interconnections were fascinating, and the twins had devoted their life's work to understanding and preserving their heritage.

Because their family was so wealthy, Nicholas and Levi had never needed to work traditional jobs. They had devoted one hundred percent of their adult lives to their studies and flown through their undergraduate and postgraduate programs. At the ripe old age of thirty, they were world-renowned in their fields.

They were also bachelors. Dating and marriage had barely crossed their minds. They joked they'd have to find girls who were also identical twins, loved traveling to archaeological sites in Mesoamerica, and didn't mind microwave meals and long nights of research. In other words, they'd be bachelors forever.

The bike rack beside the door to the Tozzer Anthropology Building, where they shared an office, was sparsely populated this early in the morning. They locked their bikes, and Nicholas held open the door for his brother, who unhooked the strap from his bike helmet as they began the three-story trek up the stairs.

"Man, I hope I don't look as ridiculous as you do with your sweaty helmet head," Nicholas said, chuckling as he removed his own helmet. He ran his hand through his thick hair, trying to straighten out the flyaways and fluff the parts that were matted down.

"We're identical twins," Levi said. "If I look ridiculous, you look ridiculous."

"Good thing I don't have any meetings this morning." Nicholas turned at the first landing, his legs still strong even after their bike ride. He was proud of their commitment to maintaining an active lifestyle, a requirement if they were going to be ready at a moment's notice if someone needed them at an archaeology dig.

"I thought you said you were meeting with a grad student." Levi had no trouble keeping up as they turned the corner at the final landing, and they almost seemed to race up the last section of stairs.

"Yeah, but he won't care what I look like," Nicholas said, pushing his brother out of his way, his spirit of competition kicking into high gear during those last few stairs. Just as he pushed open the heavy door to the third-floor hallway, he said, "No one cares what I look like."

"I care." A sultry voice startled him as he entered the hallway.

Nicholas stopped short when he noticed the gorgeous blond leaning against the wall next to the nameplate near the door to his office. Her blue eyes danced with amusement, and Nicholas was caught in her gaze as his brother plowed into him.

She chuckled but didn't move from where she stood with her arms crossed. Her professional Navy button-down dress shirt and khaki slacks were so different from the jeans and T-shirts worn by the college kids. She had a sport coat draped over her folded arms and computer bag at her feet.

"Becky?" Nicholas shook off his stupor. "I mean, Dr. Benson. What are you doing in Massachusetts?"

Chapter Two

Treasure Hunting

"Nice to see you too, Nick... I mean Dr. Stephenson." Becky pushed away from the wall, leaving her computer bag resting next to the door to the office Nicholas shared with his brother. Either she had no idea how beautiful she naturally was, or she knew darn well how her playful grin affected him.

As he'd imagined a million times in his days as a grad student, he longed to remove the clip that held her long, blonde hair in an elegant twist and watch the locks of gold fall heavily and rest on her shoulders. He watched it happen once, when she thought no one was in the computer lab.

Nicholas had felt like a stalker standing in the doorway to the computer lab late that night. He thought he had the building to himself and found her in the corner, completely engrossed in whatever remote sensing data analysis she was running.

She had stretched and yawned, then unclipped her hair and let it fall. She moaned—actually moaned—in relief. That hair twist had to be weighty on her neck, and he wondered why she never left it down. She always had to be so professional, so polished. She never let her guard down, or her hair. A shame.

After gawking like a nervous schoolboy for a few minutes, Nicholas had turned and left the computer lab. He couldn't even remember what project he'd planned to work on that evening. He was madly, passionately in love with his advisor's teaching assistant, who was completely off-limits.

He'd gone home that night and headed straight for the workout gym in the dorms, lifting weights and riding the stationary bike and then finally donning his swimsuit for a dozen laps in the pool. What he needed that night was a cold shower. He never even told his brother what had happened, and he told Levi everything.

But Becky wasn't a grad assistant anymore, and he wasn't reliant on her approval for a passing grade in Digital Imaging. They both had postdoctoral educations, they both taught at major universities, and they were both top in their respective fields. She was a peer. And she was even more beautiful than his childish fantasies remembered.

When she'd graduated with her PhD in Geography & Environment from Boston University, he'd lost touch and had almost pushed her to the back of his mind as a dream that was never within reach to begin with. He never thought he'd see her again. Yet here she stood, waiting for him to lift his gaping jaw and regain his ability to speak.

Levi cleared his throat. "Uh... Dr. Stephenson, would you like to introduce me to your... friend?"

"Sorry, yes." Nicholas glanced at his brother "Dr. Stephenson, this is Dr. Benson."

"I gathered that." Levi reached out a hand to Becky. "How exactly do you know each other?"

"Nick used to flirt mercilessly with me when I was his professor's grad assistant way back in the day."

"I did *not* flirt with you." Nicholas coughed and could feel his face and neck heating in an embarrassing rash.

"Okay, he didn't flirt, more like drooled over me."

"That's closer to the truth. I never got the nerve to speak a full sentence to you without sounding like a complete idiot."

"Which is laughable since he's probably the only guy I've ever met who is smarter than I am."

"According to IQ tests, I'm even smarter than my brother." Levi wiggled his eyebrows with a playful smirk and wrapped his arm around Nicholas's shoulder.

"And he's modest too." Nicholas shrugged out from under Levi's arm and stepped forward to lead Becky toward the door to their office. "Come on in. As you can see from the door placard, this is the very small office I share with my twin brother, who apparently is smarter than I am."

Becky giggled like a girl. "This playful side of you is refreshing, Nick. You've grown up since I saw you last."

"I had to catch up to you." Nicholas cleared off the chair beside his desk, setting aside the stack of books he kept there to deter anyone from sitting too close and invading his personal space.

"You could never catch up to me," she teased as she sat. "I'll always be two years older than you, but I like your confidence."

"Maturity has nothing to do with age." Nicholas found himself less nervous around Becky the longer they teased one another. He pulled his desk chair closer to her chair, leaned down to eye level, allowing himself to flirt a little more. "What brings you over to the East Coast? I know you didn't come all this way just to see me."

"Actually, I did." She turned around to glance at Levi, whose desk faced their direction. "Both of you."

"See, now I was just starting to feel special," Nicholas teased. "You had to go and bring my brother into the conversation."

"She needed to meet the smarter half of the geek twins." Levi pulled a chair over to squeeze in beside Becky. "How can I be of assistance, Dr. Benson, or may I call you Becky?"

"I'll think about it." She rested her finger against her lips as if in deep thought. Lucky finger. Now all he could think about was her lips. "For now, I need your linguistics expertise."

"See that, Dr. Stephenson. She needs an expert." Levi leaned over and nudged Nicholas in the arm.

"I need an archaeology expert too." Becky glanced at Nicholas. "And I need you both to pack up and come with me to Guatemala for a treasure hunt."

Chapter Three

Unusual Treasure Map

"Treasure hunt?" Nicholas gulped. Not what he'd expected this conservative, strait-laced professor to say. "What kind of treasure are you talking about?"

"The kind that rewrites history," Becky said. "The kind that changes the way archaeologists view the landscape forever. The kind that opens your eyes to new discoveries that have been hidden beneath a shroud of vegetation for thousands of years."

"You have my attention, Dr. Benson." Nicholas shoved aside his desire to flirt, tempted by the alluring pursuit of knowledge.

"She had me at treasure hunt," Levi said, leaning on his elbow, chin in his hand.

"Are either of you familiar with LiDAR?" She waited, but they both shook their heads. "No? Do you at least know what I do for a living?"

"Don't you teach at the University of Houston?" Nicholas creased his brow.

"I was recently recruited into their consortium of experts at the National Center for Airborne Laser Mapping, or NCALM."

"You always had a thing for remote sensing." Nicholas remembered the way her eyes lit up while talking about aerial photographs and digital imaging. "Congratulations on your new position."

"For once I admit ignorance on this one," Levi said. "Explain your job to me like I'm an undergrad."

"Our team flies an airplane over the tree canopy, firing billions of laser pulses down to the ground where they bounce back, and we capture them using high-tech scanning equipment." Her voice took on a sweet, teasing lilt that had Levi blinking his eyes in a daze.

"I think I'm in love with you," Levi said, his chin never leaving his hand where his elbow still rested on the edge of Nicholas's desk. "Will you marry me?"

"Now you understand why I needed so many cold showers during graduate school," Nicholas said.

"You never mentioned that." Levi still hadn't taken his eyes off Becky. "Can you say that again? Billions of laser pulses and high-tech scanning equipment?"

"I'll do even better than that and tell you how we use the speed of light to measure how much time it takes the pulse to go from the airplane to the ground and back up again to measure how *big* things are."

"Big?" Levi gulped.

"You know, the *size* of the trees and the buildings and stuff."

"Size matters, I'm sure." Levi nodded with enthusiasm.

"Especially when we *strip* away all the reflections from vegetation to reveal just the *bare jungle floor*." She leaned closer to Levi, and Nicholas fought the need to laugh at his brother.

"Stop it, Becky, you're gonna give him a heart attack." Nicholas chuckled.

"I'm givin' 'im somethin'." Becky sat back and folded her arms across her chest with a smirk.

"But seriously, back up a sec," Nicholas said. "Are you saying that you're using spectral analysis to remove the vegetation from the image to display the ground beneath the trees?"

"That's exactly what I'm saying." Her smirk turned into a full out grin. "You wanna see?"

"Yeah," both guys said at once.

"Dr. Stephenson?" A young man poked his head in the door, backpack over one shoulder and a skateboard tucked under his other arm.

In unison, both brothers answered again. "Yes?"

"Oh, you guys are creepy," Becky said. "How can you stand to share an office?"

"I don't understand the question." Levi returned his gaze to Becky.

"Sorry, got distracted talking to an old friend." Nicholas stood to shake hands with his grad student, having forgotten they had an appointment this morning to discuss his thesis project. "Hey, Dr. Stephenson, could you take Dr. Benson on a quick tour of the department while I give my full attention to my student, and then perhaps the three of us can take an early lunch to view that data analysis."

"I'd be more than happy to." Levi stood and offered Becky his hand to help her from her chair.

Becky accepted Levi's hand but pouted at Nicholas. "Don't take *too* long, Dr. Stephenson. I can't wait to show you what I've got."

"You are going to be the death of me, Dr. Benson." Nicholas felt his voice drop an octave, and his heart raced.

"I can't kill you yet, Dr. Stephenson. I need your expertise in archaeology for my treasure hunt." With that, she turned and allowed Levi to lead her from the room.

Nicholas bumped his head against the cinderblock wall and moaned.

"Your girlfriend's hot, Dr. Stephenson."

He'd almost forgotten his student was still in the room. Oops. "Yeah, well, she's not my girlfriend."

"Yet..." the little punk said.

"Anyway, about your thesis project." Nicholas walked around and sat at his desk, waving his hand for his student to take a seat.

The entire time he was trying to listen to the student's proposal, all Nicholas could think about was that one magic word. *Yet.*

Chapter Four

LiDAR

B ecky took Levi's request seriously when he asked her to explain her work to him as if he were an undergrad. "Everything we view, either with the naked eye, or through a lens or image, has a spectral signature. When you project all the signatures at once, they become a rainbow of color, similar to a prism. The technique called LiDAR—or Light Detection and Ranging—is like an x-ray to see the landscape without a chosen range on that spectrum of color. In our case, we're getting rid of the vegetation to see the ground below."

"But that whole area is just a jungle. Isn't it?" Nicholas tried to visualize that section of Guatemala. There were trees as far as the eye could see. Even from the ground, the forest was so dense a person could hardly cut a footpath, much less drag equipment to start an archaeology dig.

"Imagine flying over a small city that's covered in clouds." Becky's voice filled with the wonderment of new discovery. "All you'd see are clouds, right? Now imagine flying over that same city without the clouds and seeing all the buildings. Strip away all the clouds from the jungles of Guatemala and realize there is a city underneath."

"But there's nothing there. Explorers have looked for archaeological sites in that region for years. There's just a handful of buildings, ancient temples, pyramids, that kind of thing."

"Imagine flying over New York City with low cloud cover and seeing just the tip of the Empire State Building and then removing the clouds and seeing that what you thought was one building is actually an entire city. That's what they're finding in Guatemala. Everywhere."

"Everywhere?"

"Imagine removing the cloud cover from the entire East Coast and realizing what you thought was a couple of buildings is actually a city that spans from Boston down through New York City, Philadelphia, Baltimore, Washington D.C. and beyond."

"A megalopolis." Nicholas knew enough about urban geography to understand if one metropolis, like New York City, is too close to another metropolis, like Philadelphia, they are no longer seen as two metropolises; they are a megalopolis. What she was saying was mind blowing. There weren't any cities in the jungles of Guatemala. "What does this have to do with archeology? And linguistics?"

"Let me start with archeology," Becky said. "What if you could see not just buildings that exist now, but buildings that existed a thousand years ago? Two thousand years ago?"

"If I didn't know how incredibly intelligent you are, I'd say you were delusional."

"Have you ever been to the archeological dig site at Tikal?"

"Of course, it's one of the most famous sites in all of Mesoamerica."

"Let me show it to you on my computer screen as an aerial image." She turned her laptop so Nicholas and Levi could see. The tree-covered jungle looked very similar to how she'd described a city covered in clouds. Several tops of pyramids stuck up through the tree canopy the same way the Empire State Building would peek up through cloud cover.

"Makes me want to go back." Nicholas felt that pull he experienced every fall. The one that made him drop everything and fly to Guatemala each winter. He and Levi had a standing agreement with the university. They never taught during the winter term because that was the best time to visit Mesoamerica, before the rainy season.

"Now, let me use LiDAR to remove the trees." The excitement in her voice told Nicholas that whatever she was going to show him was the reason she'd come all this way. With the click of her mouse, a new image emerged. An image of the same exact location minus the trees.

What appeared was a region far larger than any map he'd ever seen of Tikal, with a series of squares and lines. The image confused Nicholas at first until he realized some of those squares were located at the exact spots where the known temples were located. He also recognized the great plaza, and the causeways. But there were many more squares than there were buildings at the dig sites. He'd been to that site eight times. Those buildings didn't exist. "What *is* this, Dr. Benson?"

"Each one of those squares are foundations for buildings, some of which are no longer there." The wonderment and excitement reentered her voice. "Everything with a straight edge was definitely built by humans."

"But those buildings don't exist."

"Some do. They're just covered in trees and vines and vegetation. For others, the only thing left is a foundation."

"I'm not even sure how to react to this."

"Let's look at La Corona." Becky turned her computer back toward her and clicked a few times with her mouse, then turned the computer around again. Another famous dig site Nicholas visited every winter. She readied her mouse, and with a simple click, the image changed. "With the trees... without the trees."

"Oh my gosh... there must be thousands of them."

"Just in this 800 square mile study area, they estimate an additional 60,000 ancient structures—previously unknown Mayan cities and settlements sprawling across what was thought to be uninhabited wilderness—and that's just one little study area. It's possible there were billions of people living in this region of Mesoamerica.

"For archaeological studies in the jungle, we want to get rid of all those points that come from vegetation and just leave the ground and the ancient buildings. Once all the unwanted pulses reflected from the trees are filtered out, the data that's left allows the engineers to build a 3D model of the hidden jungle floor."

"A treasure map." Nicholas sat back in his chair, amazed.

Levi piped in. "This is overwhelming. But let's circle back to my involvement. I understand why you wanted to show this to Nicholas, but what do you need me for?"

"Brace yourself for what I'm about to show you." Becky pulled up another screen on her computer, and before she turned the laptop back around, she looked at both of them with prolonged anticipation. "This was found in an uninhabited region northwest of Tikal."

She turned her computer screen toward them again, and both brothers gasped.

Chapter Five

Tree of Life

"This mound was so pronounced there was almost a bullseye on the imagery," Becky said. "Concentric circles in a near perfect Fibonacci spiral draw closer and closer to the main temple pyramid in such a way that analysts couldn't ignore its importance. Hidden in plain sight but only visible once technology caught up to its complexity."

"Where was this found?" Nicholas leaned closer to Becky's laptop, which sat on the corner of his desk so both he and his brother could view the screen. Their office was big enough that the three of them could sit close together and not feel crowded.

"In a remote region between El Zotz and Tikal," Becky said.

"There's nothing there." Nicholas tried to shake off the feeling that everything he thought he knew dissipated like the clouds covering the Empire State Building.

"And yet there is…" Becky raised her eyebrows.

"How large an area does this cover?" Nicholas asked. "And how remote? And how did they find this?"

"One question at a time, Nick," Becky scolded. "This is so far off the beaten path—or lack thereof—it was almost as if the carvers didn't want the temple to be found."

"So how did you find it?" Nicholas was growing impatient.

"The LiDAR imagery," Becky said. "Like I said, once the vegetation was stripped away the mounds were so clear there was a bullseye from the aerial view. And here are some of the carvings all around the base of the pyramid." She clicked a few times with her mouse and photo after photo popped up with stone carvings.

"Those are some of the most complex stone carvings I've ever seen," Nicholas said.

"Has anyone tried to translate the carvings yet?" Levi examined the computer screen as if he could decipher the symbols without the use of any codex. He probably could. "There are so many of them."

"Do you recognize the language?" Nicholas asked, baiting his brother. No doubt he already had a few ideas of what the rock carvings depicted.

"Of course. It's primitive, but recognizable."

"I knew you were the correct person to recruit for this project." Becky was almost bouncing in her seat, gazing at Levi with such affection that Nicholas was jealous of his brother. Even as competitive as they were, envy between them was rare. He shook off the jealousy and pulled himself back on track.

"How soon can we leave?" Levi pulled his eyes away from the computer screen to gaze at Becky.

"I'm sure you'll need to finish your semester before you run off with a team of archaeologists. Am I correct, Dr. Stephenson?" She spoke to Levi but winked at Nicholas.

"Yeah, I guess." Levi's shoulders fell. "Can I study the imagery some more?"

"Not until you feed me," she said. "I flew in late last night and took an Uber straight from my hotel without eating this morning."

"We can settle at the café across the street," Nicholas suggested. "Dr. Benson can eat while Dr. Stephenson escapes into an ancient world the rest of us can't decipher, and I'll ride my bike up the hill to retrieve my car and come back for you."

"*Our* car," Levi grumbled. "Not that I've ever driven it."

"I sense a hint of contention..." she raised her eyebrows with a playful glint.

"You'll understand when you see my baby." Nicholas wiggled his eyebrows.

"He won't let me drive it even though I paid for half."

"I'm older." Nicholas fell back on his usual argument.

"I'm smarter," Levi reminded him.

"I'm better looking." Nicholas winked at Becky.

"We're identical twins." Levi's argument was impossible to dispute.

"Becky, you decide," Nicholas said. Both guys turned to her with expectant expressions.

"I think I'm going to need to witness said vehicle before making any judgements." Her teasing lilt sent shivers up Nicholas's spine.

Nicholas leaned closer to her, meeting her gaze with what he hoped was smoldering intensity. "You two head across the street for some lunch, and I'll ride up the hill to bring my car. Then we'll leave my brother at home, and you and I can go for a drive and get reacquainted after all this time."

"Hey, you can't just leave me at home. I also deserve to get acquainted with Becky, I mean, Dr. Benson."

"I'll tell you what, Dr. Stephenson." Becky addressed Levi. "I'll leave you with access to all the files on my laptop, and you can spend the afternoon deciphering ancient text while I spend the afternoon flirting with your brother."

Nicholas smirked at Levi, and he scowled back.

"Fine, but only because you've tempted me with the one thing I care about even more than flirting with a woman. Especially one who is already enamored with my brother."

"Would you care to escort me to the café, Dr. Stephenson?" Becky asked, closing her computer and sliding it into its case.

"Of course, Dr. Benson." Levi rose from his chair and held out his arm, resigned to his fate.

"I'll meet up with the two of you in about twenty minutes." Nicholas grabbed his messenger bag and bike helmet, locked the office door behind them, and watched as his brother chatted casually with the lovely Rebecca Benson on their way to the elevator.

Nicholas turned the other direction toward the stairway leading down to where his bike was locked. He wondered at how quickly this day had shifted course. How quickly his life was destined to shift course. He bound down the stairs with a spring in his step and a soft smile on his face.

Chapter Six

Holy Lamborghini

The ride up the hill was arduous, especially racing to his condo in the heat of day rather than casually wandering home enjoying the cool of the evening. Time for a quick shower, or Becky wouldn't want to spend the afternoon in his car. Not that he expected intimacy on the day they'd met again for the first time in years, but he took a minute to run a quick razor across his stubble and brushed his teeth. Silly.

Slipping into the soft leather seat of his Lamborghini, Nicholas almost moaned with pleasure. Maybe that was his misdirected desire for the beautiful woman who would soon join him in the passenger seat.

He felt invincible shifting gears and flying down the switchbacks of the narrow roads, hoping he didn't encounter any police in these quiet residential neighborhoods. All he would need to do is suggest the officer take a moment to sit behind the wheel and maybe take a spin and the guy would be so starstruck he'd forget how many miles per hour Nicholas had been traveling over the speed limit.

Nicholas slowed as he neared campus and circled the buildings before finding a vacant spot close enough to the café to see his baby from the window. Paranoid? Yeah, just a bit. Justified? Yep. He set the car alarm and jogged across the street to meet up with Becky and Levi.

Even though the two distracted professors were tucked in a booth in the back corner, Nicholas sat at a table near the window and waved them over to join him.

While Becky creased her brows in confusion, Levi gathered the computer and his bagel, and headed toward the table in the front of the café.

"Why are we moving?" Becky asked, grabbing her briefcase and croissant sandwich.

"He won't let his baby out of his line of sight." Levi's matter-of-fact statement included his acceptance.

"Holy Lamborghini," Becky said, lowering into the chair beside Nicholas. "I can see why." Her jaw hung open, and her eyes never left the candy-apple-red Lamborghini Urus parked across the street as she took a bite of her sandwich.

"No need to rush your lunch. I won't leave without you." Nicholas lowered his voice and bumped her shoulder gently. "I'm going to grab a sandwich. You keep an eye on my car."

"Okay." Distracted, she took another bite.

He hurried to order his usual grilled chicken panini and slipped back into the seat beside Becky. "So, Dr. Benson, what have you been up to the past seven years since you finished your PhD? You married? Kids? Boyfriend? Girlfriend? Significant other? Still pining after this hot guy who used to drool over you in the computer lab during grad school?" Nicholas took a bite of his panini, passing the conversational baton.

Becky threw her head back and laughed. "No, I've never been married, haven't really had time for a significant other—male or female. I spend my days in my labs doing research and analysis; spend my evenings eating microwave meals in front of my computer, conducting more research and analysis; and get far too little sleep."

"Do you have a twin sister?" Levi looked up from his focus on the laptop.

"Sadly, no. Not all of us are able to duplicate ourselves and accomplish twice the work of mere mortals." She turned toward Nicholas. "As for still pining over certain hot geeks from my grad school days, that is something we'll have to discuss when we have a little more... privacy."

Nicholas gulped and lowered his voice. "I never said anything about said grad student being a *geek*."

"Are you disputing the title?" Her eyes smoldered.

"Absolutely not." His words had taken on a husky intensity he couldn't hold back.

"Would the two of you please leave?" Levi never looked up from the computer, but his words held annoyance. "Your foreplay is making me want to puke."

Nicholas and Becky both sat up, leaning away from each other. He didn't argue Levi's request but didn't want to abandon him. "How are you going to get home?"

"The same way I got here." Levi pointed across the street. "My bike is locked to that rack."

"What about my computer?" Becky asked.

"I have my messenger bag right here." Levi lifted the bag from the seat by his side. "I'll take good care of your laptop and meet you guys at the condo in a few hours... if you don't wind up back at Dr. Benson's hotel room, in which case I'll see you in the morning. Or afternoon. Or whenever you come up for air."

"Very funny." Nicholas stood and offered a hand to help Becky up, savoring the jolt of heat that rushed through his core at the power of her connection. Hotel room? Yeah... no. He'd never even been brave enough to kiss a girl. She was right about him being a geek. Still, geeks have feelings too. Really strong feelings. He needed to get his mind out of the gutter and take her for a drive. On a nice country road. Not to her hotel. He held up his keys. "Ready?"

She boldly threaded her fingers through his as they crossed the street, and he didn't complain. He clicked the key fob and woke up his baby, then held open the passenger door for the spunky professor who was going to bring him to his knees. The wonderment in her eyes as she settled into the leather bucket seat was worth all $270,000 of this purchase.

Nicholas hurried around to the driver's seat and drew in a whiff of the new car smell, which now held a hint of whatever perfume Becky was wearing. Yeah, he could get used to having her in his car.

"Your brother's very fun to tease." Becky's tone had changed now that she wasn't trying to make Levi jealous.

"At least he's finally resolved himself to the notion that you're not interested." Nicholas slipped on a pair of shades and carefully backed out of his parking spot.

"I don't know. He is kind of cute. Looks just like this guy I used to have a crush on during graduate school."

"Yeah?" Nicholas grinned as he shifted into drive and forced himself to keep his speed down through campus. "Tell me about this cute guy from grad school."

"Well, he was so shy around me that he could hardly put a sentence together. But I knew he was only shy around *me* because I watched him from afar and heard him talking to others when he didn't know I was nearby. He was so intelligent it was intimidating, but he was so kind to everyone that no one was really intimidated. And the work he submitted for assignments was near perfect. Always."

"I'm far from perfect." Nicholas cleared his throat and lowered his voice, no longer teasing.

"I haven't been able to stop thinking of you all these years later," she said. "I've followed your career. You, and your brother's."

"Yeah?"

"Between the two of you, you're published in so many scholarly journals I can hardly keep up."

"We have no life outside of our research," Nicholas explained. "It's easy to get published when you're competing against guys who have wives and kids and other jobs. Plus, like you said earlier, we're able to duplicate ourselves by working together."

"That's how I knew to contact you."

"And here I was starting to think you liked me for my looks and intelligence and hot car."

"Darn, you found me out."

"I hope you know Levi was just kidding about the hotel room. He knows I would never do that."

"I knew he was teasing."

"I've never even kissed a woman."

"Nick, you're thirty years old." Her jaw hung open. "What other thirty-year-old man hasn't kissed a woman?"

"Uh... the one who looks just like me and is drooling over your laptop."

"We're going to need to remedy this travesty." Becky laughed.

"You're going to kiss my brother?" Nicholas feigned shock.

"No, silly guy." She pushed his shoulder. "I'm going to kiss *you*."

"Should I pull the car over right now?" Nicholas teased. He crossed the Charles River and merged onto Interstate 90 heading toward the coast.

"Nah, you've waited thirty years. I think you can wait a few more minutes until we arrive wherever it is you're taking me."

"I'm taking you to the closest thing we have to an archaeological site in this part of the country. I hope you don't mind a quick drive."

"How long is quick?"

"Forty-five minutes."

"Forty-five minutes in a sports car with one of the smartest men I've ever met, who also happens to be really hot and has a crush on me. Hmm... let me think about it."

"You're cute." Nicholas chuckled and lifted Becky's hand to intertwine their fingers, still in shock that she was back in his life after all these years. "You know what? I think I *will* let you kiss me today. That sounds like fun."

As they wound their way south toward the Atlantic coast, banter was light and playful, getting to know each other as adults and peers, interspersed with comfortable pauses of silence.

"Ah, I forgot we have to take a charter over to the island." Nicholas pulled into the parking lot at the end of the peninsula of Hull, Massachusetts. "I hope you're not averse to hopping onto a boat."

"I'm game." She exited the vehicle without waiting for him to come around and open the door for her.

Nicholas reminded himself to be a chivalrous gentleman when possible while respecting her boundaries as a strong, independent woman. He extended a hand, inviting her to connect. She did and his heart soared again.

He paid the owner of Charter Island Tours to take them over to Lovells Island and wait there for them while they did a little sightseeing. Once on the island, they paid to have a driver take them to Fort Standish, one of the earliest fortifications in the modern defenses of Boston Harbor. Once used as a fort and gun emplacement, most of the buildings were now spalled and crumbling.

"Not exactly a thousand years old," Nicholas apologized. "But an impressive example of ruins nonetheless."

They walked around the ruins for a little while, discussing how the exploration would play out in Guatemala. They would have a team of experts to cut through the dense forest and obtain all the information they could while camping there for the winter, the only time of year when the deluge of rain slowed down and temperatures lowered into the seventies and eighties. There were nearby indigenous tribes, who would understandably be upset to have the scientists poking around one of the sites they considered to be sacred. Once the team of scientists returned to their respective universities, they would conduct analyses to make sense of the collected data.

Nicholas halted the conversation when they rounded the corner of the fort to face the Atlantic Ocean and stood in a secluded location. This was the perfect place. He leaned his back against the crumbling concrete wall and pulled Becky to himself.

Her face grew stoic. She must have known exactly why he had stopped.

"There's something I've wanted to do for years," Nicholas said, his voice low and husky. Slowly, to avoid startling her, he unclipped that which was holding her elegant twist. The golden locks fell, and she shook out her hair, letting it fall onto her shoulders. He lowered his voice even further, almost to a whisper. "You're so beautiful, Rebecca."

Without any further preamble, she leaned forward. He pulled himself away from the wall, and they met in a soft, mildly passionate kiss. Fireworks must have exploded over his head because a jolt of energy soared through his body, awaking inner desires he hadn't realized he'd been suppressing.

This woman was everything Nicholas had dreamed about and more. He couldn't wait to spend the winter in her presence. They kissed for several long minutes before driving down to the boat and riding back to the peninsula for the forty-five-minute drive home.

Chapter Seven

Burning Books

"That didn't take you long." Levi didn't look up from the computer or take his hand off his mouse. Scribbles of hieroglyphs covered his notepad and copies of all four known codices of the books of Mayan hieroglyphs sat open on the kitchen table. "Feeling better?"

"Levi, don't be a jerk." Nicholas held Becky's hand as they strode across the open room of the condo he shared with his twin. "We just went for a drive down to Fort Standish and walked around the ruins for a while, talking." *And kissing*. He didn't say that part out loud.

"What are these?" Becky leaned over the Madrid Codex, which contained a wealth of information on astrology and divinatory practices. The codex identified the various Mayan gods and reconstructed the rites, Mayan crafts, pottery, weaving, and hunting.

"These are some of the few collections of pre-Columbian Mayan hieroglyphic texts known to have survived the book burnings by the Spanish clergy during the sixteenth century." Levi finally glanced up from his work with an almost panicked expression, as if he wanted to snap at Becky not to touch his research.

Nicholas wasn't worried. Becky was a scientist like the twins. Scientists knew not to move so much as a page in another scientist's research design.

"Who would be cruel enough to burn books?" Becky feigned horror.

"Apparently the Spanish clergy of the sixteenth century," Levi said with sarcastic grumbling. "They considered them pagan. The written language of the Maya was nearly eradicated by the Spanish while trying to convince the *savages* to convert to Christianity."

"You'd think that would be the opposite of helpful," Becky said.

"It's a miracle any of this writing survived," Levi said. "The Maya were a highly literate culture. They wrote on bark paper or deerskin, using reed pens and conch shells as ink wells. Theirs was a rich and complex system of hieroglyphics similar to those used in Egypt."

"Do you see why he thinks he's smarter than me?" Nicholas stage-whispered to Becky.

"He *is* smarter than you," she whispered back. "He proposed within five minutes of meeting me. You still haven't even asked me on a date."

"How about if I spend the whole winter with you," Nicholas suggested. "Would that be a long enough date for you?"

"I suppose."

Levi grinned. "I plan to lay wagers with the rest of the team of archaeologists about how soon the two of you will be sleeping in the same tent."

"Very funny," Nicholas grumbled.

"Ah, come on, Nick." Becky stepped closer and laid her hands on his chest. As if by instinct, Nicholas found his arms wrapped around her waist. "I'm going to be the only female on the team. I'll be all alone in that dark tent and will need a strong man to keep me safe and warm."

"Yep, I give you three days, a week at the most," Levi said.

"Am I allowed to get in on the wager?" Becky asked, turning to Levi and blinking her eyes with contrived innocence.

"You traitorous vixen." Nicholas shook his head in resignation of his fate. "What am I going to do with you?"

"I can think of a few things…" Her voice trailed off, and she bit her lower lip.

"I thought I asked the two of you to go spend some time at Dr. Benson's hotel room," Levi said. "You're distracting me from my research."

"We'll stop." Becky pulled herself away from Nicholas's arms. He felt her absence as if he were a toddler and someone had yanked away his security blanket. She sat too close to Levi on one of the kitchen chairs. "Tell me more about Mayan linguistics. That is what I hired you for, right?"

"Okay, so, Mayan inscriptions are found on standing stone slabs called stelae, or horizontal stones called lintels, sculpture, pottery, plus the few surviving Mayan books, or codices." Levi was back in game mode, his excitement contagious. "The Mayan system of writing contains more than 800 characters, including some that are hieroglyphic and other phonetic signs representing syllables. The hieroglyphic signs are pictorial—meaning they're recognizable pictures of real objects such as animals, people, and things from daily life."

Levi carefully pulled the book she had been asking about closer.

"The Madrid Codex dates from the fifteenth century and was made of fig-bark paper folded like an accordion, with a cover made from jaguar skin." Levi pointed to another one of the books. "The Dresden Codex probably dates from the eleventh or twelfth century and contains astronomical calculations with surprising accuracy.

"The Paris Codex was discovered in 1859 in an obscure corner of the Bibliothèque Nationale in Paris and was just torn wrappings of a manuscript and is probably slightly older than the Madrid Codex. Last but not least was the Grolier Codex, discovered in 1971 and dates to the thirteenth century."

"This is almost as exciting as making out on the beach." Becky glanced up at Nicholas with innocent eyes.

"You guys made out on the beach?" Levi's jaw gaped. "Isn't that moving a little fast for having just gotten reacquainted after years apart?"

"It was long overdue," Nicholas said. "And it was more like on the protected side of the ruins, not really *on* the beach."

"Semantics." Becky waved her hand dismissively. She turned back to Levi. "You were saying?"

Levi sighed with exaggerated frustration. "Archaeologists painstakingly decoded the Mayan's written language and published the manuscripts. And here they are."

"Without linguists," Nicholas interrupted, "archaeologists would simply be playing in the sandbox, searching for bones and pottery fragments."

"The two of you work well together," Becky said.

"That we do." Nicholas held out his hand for Levi to give him a fist bump.

"We'd each be lost without the other," Levi agreed.

Nicholas and Levi had always believed they'd be bachelors forever. Now, as Nicholas looked at this gorgeous woman at his side, his paradigm shifted, and a new future seemed to come into focus. He wondered how this new perspective would change the relationship with his twin.

Chapter Eight

Gender Roles

"We'll leave from Houston with my boss, Dr. Timothy Cathcart, who is the Excavation Director." Becky's suggestion made perfect sense, seeing as how Timothy was the main financier and person responsible for pretty much everything. "It's just over a two-hour flight from Houston to Cancun as the crow flies over the Gulf of Mexico."

"Which would be a really long flight for a crow." Levi scooped a large bite of noodles onto perfectly positioned chopsticks and lifted the bite to his mouth.

"We used to have family in that area," Nicholas said, holding his bite of orange chicken a few inches away from his face until he finished his thought. "Mostly in Puerto Aventuras just south of Cancun."

"Well, we won't be staying in Cancun for long," Becky said. "There won't be time for sightseeing. We have a four-and-a-half-hour flight to the Mundo Maya International Airport in Flores."

"And Flores is where base camp is located, right?" Nicholas remembered that from his conversation with Becky while they were walking on the beach. But he was too distracted by that kiss to remember everything clearly. Plus, Levi hadn't been part of that conversation.

"Yes, that is where we'll meet the rest of the team. We'll spend a few days working through the logistics before driving up to Tikal. With a project this complex, we can't skimp on the planning."

"From an archaeologist's standpoint, this is more of an exploration than an excavation," Nicholas said. "The most important people on the team will be the field guides and cartographers. We're basically following a map that doesn't exist—outside of a computer—to a place none of us have ever been, in search of a city no one knew existed."

"You two will fit right in," Becky said. "I'm the person who will be out of my element. My remote sensing and cartography skills will come in handy, but I'm pretty useless without my computer mapping."

"Just stick with us, and we'll protect you," Levi said with a confidence Nicholas didn't feel. There were logistics Becky probably hadn't considered.

"Do you know how to pitch a tent?" Nicholas was fearful of her answer.

"I can learn..."

"Cook over an open fire? Dig your own latrine? Find and purify water? Ration your food so you don't starve?"

"So... basically you need me to become a Boy Scout." Becky chuckled nervously and gulped. "I'm in trouble, aren't I?"

"Nah, like Levi said, we'll help you. Get me the name of the site manager, and I'll find out what he already has and what we need to bring for you. We'll do some shopping while we're still in the States."

"Okay." This confident professor didn't seem so confident now that she realized there were more moving parts than she'd considered.

Nicholas thought of another aspect they'd need to address, and the subject was a little more delicate. "I don't want this to come across as sexist but having a woman with us on this expedition adds another layer to the logistics."

"How so?" Becky raised her chin in defiance. "I can do anything a man can do."

"Really? Can you whip it out and pee behind a tree? Over the six weeks we'll be traveling, will you have any periods? Those are things we don't have to deal with as guys." As Nicholas spoke, Becky's shoulders fell. "Sorry to be blunt, but this has nothing to do with what a woman can do compared to what a man can do. Women's bodies are physiologically different from men's. We have to take those things into consideration, or you're going to be miserable."

"Have you been on expeditions with women in the past?" Becky bit her lower lip, but her eyes were hopeful.

"Of course. And the site manager will be prepared for all that. I just want you to be cognizant of the challenges."

"I'll do a little more research and planning," Becky said.

"Speaking of research," Levi interrupted. "Can we get back to it and quit talking about women's bathroom habits?" He stood and gathered empty takeout containers from their Chinese food-eating frenzy. I need this kitchen table back."

"Well, I need my computer back," Becky said. "It's getting late, and I need to head over to my hotel."

"Can you share those images with me in a Dropbox or something?" Levi asked, sliding Becky's laptop toward her.

She clicked on the keyboard and mouse for a few minutes, then closed the computer down. "That should do it. You realize those are only a few snapshots with a drone, right? There will be hundreds more images once we get there and start collecting data in situ."

"I know." Levi opened his own laptop and navigated to the files. "I'm just excited to get started."

"Get through the end of your semester, and I'll have the director contact you with travel plans. Well, more accurately, his assistant will contact you."

"Sounds good." Levi was already distracted with his computer and codices.

"I'll drive you back to your hotel." Nicholas stood and grabbed his keys from the key holder near the door while Becky tucked her laptop away.

"See you in the morning, Dr. Stephenson," Levi said with a smirk.

"That joke's getting old, Dr. Stephenson." Nicholas smacked his twin lightly upside the head. "I'll see you in a little while."

"Wait until the rest of the team starts laying into you." Levi laughed, completely unapologetic. "Might as well get it over with now while you still have some privacy."

"I would apologize for my brother's rude behavior," Nicholas told Becky. "But there is no excuse for him."

"Wait until he meets the right woman," Becky teased. "Turnaround is fair play you know."

"Send her my way when you find her," Levi called after her. "Nice meeting you, Dr. Benson."

"You as well, Dr. Stephenson," she called back. "Don't stay up too late with that research."

"I'm sure I'll get more sleep tonight than you two will," Levi mumbled playfully.

"I'm so sorry." Nicholas turned on the light in the garage and shut the door, drowning out any further taunting. He opened the car door for her to climb into his Lamborghini.

"He's just saying what you're thinking." Becky brushed past him on her way to climb into the car.

"What about you?" Nicholas asked, pushing her gently against the side of the car and wrapping his arms around her waist. "What are *you* thinking?"

"The same thing you're thinking," she whispered. He highly doubted that. "I'm thinking I look forward to getting to know you better before we jump into anything physical."

"Yeah... that's exactly what I was thinking too." *Not*. "I'd better drive you back to your hotel now."

"If you insist." She pouted.

"Keep that up, and the guys won't have anything to wager." He leaned down and kissed her neck, then reluctantly pulled away and offered her his hand to help her into his car. He needed to drop her off at her hotel so he could come home and take a cold shower.

Chapter Nine

Z-E-R-O

"Let's get one thing out of the way immediately." Dr. Timothy Cathcart looked pointedly around the team of thirteen explorers. "Almost all of us in this group have PhDs and are renowned as the best of the best in our fields, so drop all pretenses and stick with first names during the entire trip. Got it?"

Everyone nodded and glanced around. None of them seemed particularly haughty or pretentious, so Nicholas wasn't worried.

"Other than our shovelbum over here." Timothy pointed at the youngest member of the team. "He's *just* a grad student."

That brought chuckles, and the man beside him ruffled the kid's hair. They looked alike. Father and son, maybe?

The small makeshift conference room at the base camp in Flores, Guatemala, wasn't much more than a few slabs of sheet metal held together with industrial nails on a wooden frame. It did little to keep out the heat or the flies. Nicholas had forgotten how much he hated this aspect of archaeology explorations and decided now would be a good time to invest in the local economy and build a more permanent structure here.

"Seriously, though, let's go around the room and get to know each other. We'll be spending the next six weeks in pretty close quarters." Timothy pointed at the younger kid again. "Matt, you want to get us started since I've already picked on you? Tell us your name, where you're from and your field of expertise, plus your title and what your role will be on this team."

"Sure." Matt sat up straighter, with more confidence than Nicholas expected. "I'm at Cornell, working on a Master of Arts in Archaeology with a concentration in Ritual and Religion. As Timothy mentioned, I'll be your field technician, aka grunt, shovelbum, digger, gopher, whatever you want to call me."

"We'll just call you Matt," Timothy said with a wink. "Welcome. Is this your first expedition?"

"Nah, my dad's been dragging me along to digs since I was old enough to carry my own fifty-pound pack." Matt smiled at the man beside him.

"Had to get him started in the family business early." The man nodded and bumped Matt's shoulder. "I go by Matthew so you all can tell us apart. At least I've got twenty-five years on him. It's gonna take a while for us to tell the twins apart." Matthew hitched his thumb to the side.

"Sorry about that." Levi shrugged. "Maybe one of us should have dyed our hair or something."

"We'll get to know you soon enough," Matthew said. "Anyway, I'm the reason Matt chose Cornell since that's where I completed my PhD in Anthropology with a concentration in archaeology. I will be serving on this expedition as your field director." Matthew turned to Levi, who sat to his left.

"Greetings. I'm Levi, the more intelligent of the Geek Twins, as proven by extensive IQ testing, my chosen field of linguistics, and the fact that I proposed to my brother's girlfriend before he even asked her on a date." Levi spouted his diatribe with a straight face, drawing more laughter than a stand-up comedian.

Nicholas met his brother's humor with a lighthearted disclaimer. "As the older of the Geek Twins—and more mature—I will *not* be held responsible for anything that comes out of my brother's mouth."

"Don't worry, Nicholas, your mouth will be regularly silenced by Dr. Benson's lips."

"Ooh! Slam!" Multiple members of the team jeered and laughed at them while Nicholas felt his cheeks flush.

"Is it hot in here?" Nicholas asked playfully, pulling at his collar.

"I feel the heat whenever you sit next to me," Becky said with a smirk.

"Good thing too," Levi said. "Because Nicholas will need a lot of cold showers over the next few weeks."

That brought more laughter, and Nicholas rolled his eyes. "Like I said, I will not be held responsible for him."

Levi pulled his wallet from his back pocket, slipped out a dollar bill, and tossed it to the middle of the table. "Anyone else want to lay a wager of how many days until I no longer have a roommate in my tent and Becky is no longer afraid of the dark?"

Amid laughter and jeers, most of the guys threw a dollar on the table.

Becky leaned closer and whispered to Nicholas, "What if I'm afraid of the dark tonight?"

"Unless you want to find a magistrate this afternoon, you might want to get a flashlight." Since his lips were so close to her ear, Nicholas kissed her neck, and she giggled.

"Just to make this wager fair"—Levi started numbering pieces of paper from one to eleven and handed them out—"take a slip of paper and write your name on it. If they hold out past eleven, we'll start over."

"Weren't we discussing fields of study?" Nicholas asked. "Safe topics like logistics and job titles, responsibilities at camp. That kind of thing?"

"Your responsibility each evening is to help Becky get her tent set up properly." Levi patted him on the back.

"Anyway…" Nicholas couldn't fight a grin. "I'll go next. My name is Nicholas, and I currently teach at Harvard but completed my PhD at Boston University with a degree in anthropology. I will be serving as the team's environmental archaeologist and my very irreverent twin will be our linguist." Nicholas turned to Becky, passing the spotlight.

"I'm Rebecca, and I currently work at the University of Houston at the National Center for Airborne Laser Mapping. I too completed my PhD at Boston University, studying Geography & Environment. What else?" Becky scratched her chin. "Oh, and I'm engaged to Levi and sleeping with Nick, so this should be an interesting adventure." That brought more laughter.

"Would you like me to trade chairs so you can sit between us, darling?" Nicholas asked playfully.

"Did the three of you know each other while at Boston?" Matthew asked.

"Becky and I did," Nicholas said.

"I was his TA in the GIS lab."

"Completely off-limits." Nicholas hid his sarcasm behind a fake cough.

"Not anymore." Becky's singsong declaration was followed by a flirty smile.

"I give 'em four days," one guy said.

"Two."

"Can I change my number? There's no way they're making it to eight."

"Shoot, I got eleven, what are you complaining about?"

Nicholas leaned closer to Becky and stage-whispered, "It's not too late to get on the plane and head back to the States."

"Heck no!" Becky pulled out a dollar bill and tossed it into the middle with everyone else's. Then she grabbed one of the extra pieces of paper Levi had torn apart and made a show of writing out the word Z-E-R-O and tossed that on the pile. "Game on."

Nicholas laughed heartily and laid his head on the table, peeking up at her. "You are in so much trouble."

She just grinned back at him, and Nicholas felt his heart melt along with his resolve. He was the one in trouble, and they all knew it.

Chapter Ten

Balancing Chemical Equations

"Want to go for a walk?" Nicholas leaned closer to Becky but didn't need to speak too quietly because the chatter in the conference room was more a post-meeting circle of smaller conversations. He stood and offered his hand, helping Becky from her seat.

As if their earlier taunts hadn't garnered enough teasing, being the first to leave the table and leaving together, set the group off again.

"Sneaking off together already?" Matthew asked.

"Dr. Benson doesn't want to lose the bet," Levi said. "She's got a lot invested in tonight's adventures."

"You get her pregnant, and I'm holding you in breach of contract for stealing one of my best faculty members," Timothy called from across the table.

"Gentlemen, we are going for a *walk* together." Nicholas nodded regally to the group. "I may not have a degree in physiology, but I'm pretty sure that won't get her pregnant." He escorted Becky from the room.

"Goodnight, guys!" Becky called over her shoulder. "Hold on to that money for me!"

"You're adorable, you know that?" Nicholas kissed her temple. He led her onto the dusty street that ran alongside the base camp and toward downtown Flores. The lights from the city lit the sky in an urban glow that only penetrated a short distance before being swallowed in a blackness speckled with a million diamonds. A car honked in the distance, and a dog nearby barked incessantly for no apparent reason.

"They're all too easy to tease." As she'd done when they first rode in his Lamborghini, as soon as they were alone, Becky shifted from flirting with the guys to a mature lady. "Don't worry, I'm not going to spend the evening trying to seduce you."

"That's good, because I was kind of hoping to save that until after we're married." He wondered how she'd react. When she'd learned he was thirty and never been kissed, she'd laughed at him. By deductive reasoning, she would have already figured out that he was still a virgin. Would his desire to wait until marriage be a deal-breaker? He hoped not, but now would be the time to get that conversation out of the way before getting too emotionally involved and having their hearts broken.

"Me too," Becky said without hesitation.

"Really?" He turned her to face him. "You're not just saying that?"

"No, I'm serious. I may flirt and goof off, but when it comes down to actually sleeping together, I really want a lifetime commitment first."

Nicholas let out the breath he'd been holding. "I figured you were going to think I was a prude and a geek."

"Well, I know you're a geek," she teased, then turned and kept walking. "I'm glad we talked about this because it's better for us to make that decision now than in the heat of the moment, ya know?"

"No, actually, I don't." Nicholas chuckled. "I've never gotten that far around the bases. I'm so inexperienced I don't even know what the bases are, unless you're comparing them to acids. Then I can tell you the coefficients to balance any chemical equation."

Becky threw her head back and laughed, seeming carefree and excited about life. "There's definitely enough chemistry between us, I'll give you that."

"See, if we were smart, we'd just sleep in the same hotel room tonight, take their money in the morning, and go out for brunch."

"Tempting... but so are you." Her contemplative whisper told its own story. "I'm not sure I want to tempt *myself* that way."

Nicholas pulled her to a stop again, the dust from the road settling in a puff around their feet. He searched her blue eyes for a moment, the waning light darkening them to nearly grey. "Rebecca Benson, I think I might fall in love with you."

"You know what I think?" She allowed herself to drift closer until their bodies were nearly touching. He waited for her to answer her own question. "I think you need to start looking for jobs near Houston."

"You think so, huh?" He tucked a lock of hair that had fallen from its clip around her ear, then boldly reached around and pulled the clip out entirely, letting her hair cascade over her shoulders. "For our wedding, I'd love for you to wear your hair down."

"Are you proposing to me, Dr. Stephenson?"

"Would you like me to propose to you, Dr. Benson?" He stepped even closer and wove his fingers into the heavy locks at the base of her neck, damp from her shower a million hours ago before two plane rides and one very long planning meeting. "How is your hair wet after all these hours?"

"Hair doesn't dry when it's tucked up in a clip. Plus, the humidity here won't allow it to dry. I'm probably sweaty and gross."

He pulled the hair off one shoulder and placed a kiss behind her ear, causing her to go limp in his arms with a soft moan. He moved to the other side and placed a kiss there as well. His voice was husky as he mumbled, "You don't smell sweaty to me... at all."

"That's good..." Her words were barely a breath. "Yeah, so, about this whole waiting for marriage thing, how committed to that notion are you?"

"About eighty percent." He kissed her neck again, then moved up her chin toward her lips. "Seventy-five, maybe." He captured her mouth in his and thought to himself, *fifty. Maybe forty-five.*

As they kissed while standing in the dusty street behind the makeshift conference room all Nicholas could think about was how quickly the numbers were falling and how good brunch would taste in the morning.

Chapter Eleven

Tikal and Beyond

Nicholas rolled over to the bittersweet feeling of waking up the following morning in the small bunk room he shared with his twin brother, Levi. On one hand, he hadn't violated his commitment to himself and to Becky that they wait until after marriage to sleep together. On the other hand, he missed the opportunity to wake up in the arms of the most incredible woman he'd ever met.

They still managed to fit in brunch together, his treat since she'd already lost the bet she'd made with the other guys on the team. A hearty meal of eggs and chorizo with handmade tortillas was delicious but hardly a substitute for the sweet kisses from the night before.

Knowing they'd be called out and accused of messing around if they so much as walked inside either of their bunk rooms, Nicholas and Becky sat up half the night talking at a picnic table in full view of the whole camp. Sure, they kissed—a lot—but nothing beyond kissing.

Even with just kissing, Nicholas was high as a kite with emotion, and Becky's eyes were glassy as if she had a secret only he could share. They were in love—head over heels, planning-the-wedding-and-naming-the-babies kind of in love. All that stood in their way was a six-week hike through the jungles of Guatemala and eleven of their colleagues. Minor inconveniences and a blink in time compared to the rest of their lives together.

Becky would play up the flirting with the rest of the team and made a show of tempting Nicholas beyond his ability to resist, yet would flip a switch into a mature lady who could discuss the philosophies of the world, politics, religion, financial planning, vacations, scientific discoveries. Nicholas loved all of her faces—the flirty, playful girl, the temptress, and the lady. She was everything he'd ever dreamed to find in a life partner, and by some stroke of luck, she loved him too.

The team spent hours each day planning and working together as a team, organizing equipment and supplies, setting up camp each evening and tearing it down each morning just as they'd do once they'd left the safety and security of Flores. They poured over maps and aerial photos and drone videos, getting as much data about the terrain as they could before hacking it apart with a machete. Finally, a week after arriving at the base camp, the site manager deemed them ready to leave and declared the following morning as Day One of the expedition.

"Are you nervous?" Nicholas asked that night while sitting at their picnic table at the center of base camp.

"A little," Becky admitted. "I mean, you know, bugs, snakes, monkeys, Mayan Aborigines."

Nicholas leaned his head back and laughed heartily. "We're not going to Australia so I'm pretty sure you won't see any Aborigines, but Mayans, sure. There might be some native tribes hiding."

"Do you think they're going to be mad at us for disturbing their sacred ground?"

"Maybe a little," Nicholas said. "We'll try to leave the site as unscathed as possible. These guys are good at what they do. All we want is to collect some data and analyze what we find."

"That makes sense." She pondered for a moment, brow creased. "Are you glad I dragged you on this adventure?"

"More than you could possibly imagine."

They slept in their bunks for the last time that night, and Nicholas was sure that would be the last time anyone would sleep in these bunks. He'd already begun the construction for a state-of-the-art research facility where future explorers could rest in comfort before trekking out into the inhospitable jungles.

He wasn't looking forward to cramming into a tent with his brother the following night. Sleeping in Becky's tent sounded better and better all the time.

The hour drive from Flores to Tikal was easy compared to braving the almost nonexistent trail into the jungle. They stopped in Tikal briefly because most of the team were Americans and had either never been there before or hadn't been back in at least a year.

Visiting the ancient ruins was surreal after knowing that its size was thousands of times larger than they'd realized just a few short months ago. The use of LiDAR to evaluate the landscape truly had changed history, as Becky had mentioned.

Nicholas stood in the center of the square in Tikal and turned slowly, gazing out into the jungle, imagining the buildings that were hidden within its trees. Some buildings were nothing but rubble on top of foundations. Others were full-sized pyramids and temples, homes, businesses.

Teams of archaeologists were tripping over each other to explore the newly discovered sites. But none of them were venturing as far into the wilderness as the eleven men and one woman who would set out with him today.

After paying homage to the great city of Tikal, the team piled into the Jeeps again and skirted the tourist areas, taking a little-used road into the jungle where a group of foresters had created a secret trail off to the south, hiding the entrance in such a way that a person would need to know the path existed in order to find it. The drivers knew to travel exactly ten miles, then stop. The only clue to the entrance was a set of GPS coordinates and intuition.

The Jeeps were parked just long enough for the team to unload their basic equipment. They would leave the explorers to travel on foot for the rest of the trek.

Bushwhacking through the dense jungle would not be easy, but the most important reason for not bulldozing hundreds of trees and creating a road was to deter looters. So far, this site was as hidden as all the other ruins that were shrouded in vegetation and only visible from the air through LiDAR.

Keeping the integrity of the ancient temple was paramount. Rarely did scientists have the opportunity to collect data in situ from an undisturbed site. Usually the ruins had been pilfered decades ago. This site was not only intact, it was sacred.

A small team of foresters had cut a path that would make the journey easier, but the cuttings didn't start until after crossing the first mound so as not to be seen from the road. Foresters had also created several cutouts just large enough to set up camp for the night. At their final destination, the foresters had cut down enough trees that the team would be able to spread out a little more and set up a more permanent worksite. Even that clearing had to be strategically hid from the air. Their goal was to keep this site invisible to anyone without LiDAR technology.

Even surrounded by twelve other scientists—one of whom was his twin brother, and one who was the woman he planned to marry—Nicholas felt very alone watching the taillights of the Jeeps disappear.

Chapter Twelve

Mound Builders

The distance up and over the first mound was almost a full day's walk. Instead of chopping down saplings and shrubs with machetes to make the trek easier—as they would do once over the first mound—they held branches out of the way for each other, creating as little trace of their path as possible to be visible from the road.

They relied heavily on GPS coordinates and compasses to maintain the correct heading, depending on faith and intuition as much as possible. Trusting that their field guide, a local man they called James, would know the proper techniques for navigating the jungles of Guatemala, the team followed his lead.

As part of their advance training, they'd all received basic cartography skills, beyond what any of them had learned in the computer lab. On this exploration, they weren't just creating their own path, they were creating a map that could someday be used by others to reach this same sacred site.

The slope of the mound was gradual, almost to the point of being invisible to the eye but was obvious on the legs. By the time they reached the apex, there was very little relief because they were too exhausted to be excited.

Gradually, they made their way down the other side of the mound, the only evidence of the slope coming from the subtle difference in the ache of their legs.

Lunch consisted of protein bars eaten on the move with the promise that their campsite would allow a tiny fire to warm up some premade meals and a few downed trees as logs to sit together as a group.

By late afternoon, the grumbling had turned to humor, especially after Becky started planning the trip to the spa that awaited them at the bottom of the hill.

"I sure hope the hot tub is ready when we get there."

"It's too hot for that tonight," Tim answered her. "Maybe the pool will be open though."

"But my sore muscles need the hot tub," Becky whined playfully. "That or a massage. Hey, which one of you guys is trained as a masseuse?"

Levi was the first to jump on that opportunity. "Nicholas graduated top ten in his massage therapy class."

"Really?" Becky turned to look at Nicholas. "I would have thought he was better than that. At least top five or top two."

"You know this from experience?" the site manager, Jonas, asked. "Maybe we should all get in line when we're done setting up our tents."

"Very funny," Nicholas said, winking at Becky and wishing he could fulfil her need for a complete rub down at the end of the evening. He wished he could fulfil her need for a lot of things at the end of the evening. He'd settle for helping set up her tent and dig her own private latrine far on the other side of the camp, away from the guys.

Now that he was in love with Becky, her comfort and security was almost paramount above his own. Anything he could do for her, he would. As independent as Becky wanted to portray herself, there was a soft heart underneath, and a vulnerability in her eyes when she spoke of her dreams for the future. He wanted to wave a magic wand and help make those dreams into their own two-person reality.

"Keep your eyes peeled for the campsite," James called out. As field guide, he was paying close attention to the compass and GPS coordinates. "The foresters may have done such a good job with camouflage we might walk right past and miss it."

"What are we looking for exactly?" Becky asked. Although she was the only person who hadn't been on an exploration before, she was not the only one experiencing this extreme travel.

The other expeditions Nicholas and his brother had been a part of were at well-known and settled camps, where tents and cabins were already available. This was extreme wilderness survival.

"Remember those photographs we looked at a few days ago?" James asked. "The foresters took images of each campsite so we would know them when we saw them."

"We looked at thousands of photographs this week," Becky said. "Remind me about some specifics."

"From this viewpoint, we're looking for pockets that seem to have fewer trees than the surrounding areas," James told her. "Once we arrive, there should be obvious patches cleared of trees and shrubs large enough to fit a tent, and not much else."

Nicholas saw the location about the same time several other people did, and a general excitement embodied their renewed enthusiasm as team members pointed and said, "Over there," and, "That's got to be it."

The team's excitement was squashed upon arriving at the prepared campsite when they discovered there was barely enough room to fit the tents. Because of the need to maintain the integrity of the tree canopy, the foresters had cut as few trees as possible.

They got to work immediately setting up tents as best they could, helping each other out as much as possible to make quick work of the task. Rain threatened the evening, so they opted out of building a fire, choosing instead to prepare for an early retreat into shelter and a healthy dinner of MREs.

Nicholas and Levi set up their tent as close to Becky's as possible in hopes she wouldn't feel as alone. Most of the team had zipped themselves into their two-man tents already but Nicholas couldn't bring himself to leave Becky.

"Nick," Levi hissed from inside their tent. "Come here."

"What?" Nicholas peered through the mesh tent flap where his brother lay on his back with his favorite Mayan codex in his hands, taking advantage of the waning light to study a book he probably had memorized.

"Get in here and grab your bedroll and backpack and take them over to Becky's tent. Nobody's going to think less of you for comforting her on a stormy night."

"Let me guess, tonight's the night you would win the bet?"

"Screw the bet. I don't want my future sister-in-law sleeping by herself in the middle of a jungle."

That was all the prompting Nicholas needed to unzip the tent he was supposed to share with his twin brother, grab his things, and brazenly move them all into his girlfriend's tent.

"Does this count as sleeping together?" Becky whispered in the dark, tucked in Nicholas's protective arms. "Have we officially lost the wager?"

"I lost that wager the first time I looked into your blue eyes." Nicholas kissed the top of her head and relished this moment. Abandoning his preplanned accommodations in favor of sleeping in Becky's tent had been the best choice he'd made in years, maybe his lifetime. "Do you mind losing the wager?"

"No. I'm just glad you're here." She snuggled closer.

"Me too. I wouldn't have been able to sleep knowing you were over here by yourself."

"What about Levi? He's by himself."

"He and I have slept in the jungle before. This is your first time."

"There's a *first time* for everything." Becky's statement had open-ended insinuations and a hint of innuendo.

"And some things are worth waiting for until the moment is right," Nicholas said definitively, not wanting either of them to let their imaginations wander.

"I look forward to the day when the moment is right." Becky sighed.

"Me too." Nicholas pulled her closer. "Now, let's get some sleep. We've got a long trek over another grueling mound again tomorrow."

Chapter Thirteen

Losing the Wager

Nicholas was surprised how quickly he fell asleep, especially lying on the hard jungle floor. Not to mention the distraction of holding in his arms the most tempting and alluring woman his wildest dreams could conjure up. He didn't stir until Becky stretched and yawned.

"Good morning, sleepyhead." Her scratchy voice poked through his fog, and Nicholas pulled her even closer.

"Stay," he mumbled. "Few more minutes." His eyes never opened, but a soft smile pulled at the corners of his mouth.

"I have to go to the bathroom," Becky said, pushing him gently away. "I've been waiting for the sun to rise so I wasn't searching in the dark for that hole in the ground you dug."

"M-kay." Nicholas reluctantly allowed his arms to release her from his clutches, and Becky scrambled to unzip the tent flaps.

He never dreamed of falling in love this hard this fast. His mind wandered back several years to the first time he saw Becky, and he realized their love story hadn't happened quickly at all.

Eight years and six months ago, he'd walked into the GIS computer lab, expecting a kid almost as geeky as himself to act as a graduate assistant. When this elegant blonde woman turned around and smiled at him, Nicholas felt his knees go weak. He could barely introduce himself he was so tongue tied.

Not only was Becky off-limits as his TA, she was out of his league. Yet she always found a reason to peek over his shoulder and ask him about his work. He never had to fake ignorance on something to request her assistance because she frequently gave him her undivided attention, almost as if she craved his closeness just as he craved hers.

He still craved her closeness.

By the time he'd mulled over the slow burn of their relationship, she returned, carrying the roll of toilet paper she kept in her backpack, which she stashed in its designated pocket and grabbed her little bottle of hand sanitizer. As she rubbed the alcohol gel into her palms, Nicholas reached for his own backpack and dug out a pack of gum.

"I refuse to allow my morning breath to deter you from returning to snuggle with me." He held up the pack of gum with a grin.

"Ooh, I'll take a piece." Becky scrambled across the bedroll they'd shared and wiggled her way back inside the sleeping blanket.

The unspoken message for each other in the gray haze of morning was of desire. Although his doctorate was in archaeology, he knew enough anatomy and physiology to remember that men's testosterone levels were comparatively higher first thing in the morning than at any other time of day.

He ignored the warning in the back of his mind that making out with Becky was a really bad idea. His mind and body were in complete disagreement about the subject.

She was making his commitment to waiting for marriage very difficult. Her hands gripped into his hair and then roamed down his shoulders and chest. When Becky rolled onto her back and pulled Nicholas on top of her, that woke him up. Completely.

"Whoa, babe, we can't do this!" Nicholas pushed her away gently but firmly, his conscience finally overpowering his body. Barely.

Staring up at the ceiling of the tent, Becky pulled her hair and growled softly. "Please?"

"No, no, no, no, no." Nicholas scrambled for his shoes, needing to put distance between them before he changed his mind.

"I'm sorry," Becky whispered. "I didn't mean to—"

"Babe, you have nothing to apologize about." Nicholas leaned over and kissed her one more time. "I want you just as much as you want me—probably more—but we need to wait."

"I know, I know." She sighed. "I can be patient."

"Soon, I promise." He placed one last tiny peck on her lips and reached for the tent zipper.

Dawn had awakened most of the team, and the guys were emerging from the cocoons of their tents, sleepy-eyed and yawning. Nicholas tried to sneak away from Becky's tent without being noticed.

"Well, well, well, what have we here?" Jeremiah, the team's finds manager clucked his tongue at Nicholas with a knowing smile. "Who wagered they'd cave by day nine? Or would this be day eight, since I'm assuming Nicholas has been in Rebecca's tent since last night. So, who wagered day eight?"

"We did not do anything last night." Nicholas held up his hands in surrender to their teasing. "I just didn't want her to be alone in the jungle."

"The wager didn't require proof of a physical relationship, just that you slept in the same tent, which seeing as how you are currently climbing out of her bed as the sun rises, I'm pretty sure we can make a reasonable assumption that you did indeed sleep in Rebecca's tent."

"I'm a billionaire," Nicholas said. "I'm pretty sure I can afford to lose a few dollars on a wager, especially if that means I get to sleep in the arms of the most incredible woman in the world."

"Wait, you're a... billionaire?" Jeremiah wasn't the only member of the team standing dumbfounded with his jaw hanging open.

"Well, our estate is worth over a billion." Nicholas waved a finger back and forth between himself and the tent where Levi still slept. "Just because we shared a couple of strands of DNA, our parents say we have to split the inheritance. I'm older so I really should get more than half."

"I'm smarter," Levi called from inside the tent. There was a flurry of activity inside as Levi made his way to the door and unzipped the tent flap. "I'm sure by the time we retire I will have invested more wisely, and my net worth will be greater."

"My net worth is already greater from the simple luxury of sleeping in the arms of the woman I love."

"And the rest of us are going to puke up our breakfast from the gooey love-fest vibe you got going on," Jeremiah said.

"No puking up breakfast," Timothy called out. "We need to hold on to all the energy we can if we're going to finish this trek before sundown. Now let's pack up these tents, clean up your campsites, and get going." As excavation director, he was in charge. His little speech spurred them all into action, and within 45 minutes, the team was on their way.

Chapter Fourteen

"Ba'ax a k'áat?"

T he second day of trekking through the jungle was both easier and more difficult. Easier because they were able to chop through the brush with machetes. They were less concerned with leaving a visible path from the road now that they were over the first mound of the spiral. More difficult because they were exhausted.

There was little in the way of conversation all day. The only communication was in working together to blaze a trail and carve a path up and over the second mound. They took turns at the point position, but with five machetes between thirteen people, they were able to switch out frequently as their arms tired.

The elation at coming upon their campsite early that evening was subdued. The more quickly they could get their tents erected, the sooner they could climb inside and collapse.

They didn't get that far.

What started as a few snapping twigs at the periphery of the camp led to the ominous feeling of being surrounded. Instinctively, everyone in the team gathered to the center of the camp, and Nicholas wrapped his arms around Becky, a futile attempt to protect her.

Native Mayans were likely nervous about these foreigners invading their land. The team knew this might happen. But knowing something in the abstract and actually experiencing an ambush were very different.

"Hello?" Timothy called out. "Is anyone out there?" There was no noise.

"Máaxech," Levi called out. "Ba'ax a k'áat?"

A beautiful young woman stepped into the clearing, startling everyone. She looked directly at Levi asking, "A t'aan maaya'ex?"

Levi nodded and answered her. "Je'el."

"What are you saying?" Nicholas asked his brother through clenched teeth. The fact that they were communicating was a good sign.

"I asked what they wanted," Levi said. "And she asked me if I understood her language. Obviously, I do. She's confused."

The woman looked around at the other members of the group, then back at Levi and said something else in her native Mayan tongue.

Levi shook his head and answered her, then translated his statement into English. "No, I'm the only person here who speaks Yucatec."

She wore a colorful textile dress, obviously tribal rather than a costume, and had her hair pulled back, intricately braided on top, and cascading down her back. A small headdress made of ornately carved wood and feathers adorned her head, not large enough to be that of a queen. A princess, maybe? Daughter of a tribal leader perhaps? She was fascinating.

"In k'aaba' Levi." Levi put his hand on his chest and then pointed to her, most likely asking her name. "Bix a k'aba?"

Her suspicious gaze darted between Levi and Nicholas, and Levi stepped closer to his twin, moving his hand between the two.

"In suku'un," Levi said. "My brother. And my friends. In nuup'o'ob" He waved his hand in a sweeping gesture to include the whole group.

"Ba'ax a k'áat?" She turned his words around, demanding to know what they wanted.

"She wants to know why we're here," Levi said to the group. "We are scientists. Chan científicos. We want to study the temple pyramid. Táak k xook le templo." He pointed in the direction the team was heading.

A startled expression crossed her face. Her wide eyes darted around the group. "Teche' ma' k'a'ana'an wojéeltik tu yo'olal le je'elo." Angry words spewed forth, loud and fast. Nicholas wondered if Levi could even translate that complicated rant.

"I think she said we're not supposed to know about the temple. Their tribe has probably been protecting the temple for generations. I need to let her know we won't hurt the temple." Levi paused to breathe, then spoke to her in a soft, placating tone. "Ma' táan k herir le templo. Táak k paakat le templo."

"Ma'. Ko'oten ojéeltbil ti in yuum." She turned around and made a motion to the others who were hiding in the jungle, out of our sight.

"She said, no, and that we need to come and meet her father." Levi turned to meet Nicholas's gaze with wide eyes. "I have a feeling we are about to meet the tribal chief."

"I have a feeling you're right," Nicholas said. "Depending on how far away the village is located, this could be a long night."

As he spoke, dozens of men with curved swords and spears surrounded their camp on all sides.

Chapter Fifteen

That's Not Food

If there was any silver lining that the team hadn't had time to set up camp before the ambush, it was that they still had their packs safely strapped to their backs. But they were hungry, tired, and most of them needed to use the bathroom. After at least an hour of following the tribal warriors, Becky finally begged Levi to ask them if they could take a break.

"Je'el u páajtal k parar biilankiltej táankab?" Levi asked the chief's daughter.

"Mina'an wichkíil."

"She says there is no bathroom," Levi told the group. "I'll ask her if we can just pee behind a tree. Lu'um? Paach junkúul che'?"

"Please." Becky stepped forward, crossing her legs and holding herself, pleading with her eyes, woman to woman.

The chief's daughter rolled her eyes. "Ma'alob. Bin." Her resigned expression was all the translation the team needed.

"Dad, get the toilet paper out of my backpack side pocket," Matt mumbled.

"Mine too." Becky turned around, offering her pack to Nicholas for easier access. "And come with me. I don't want to be in the jungle by myself."

The guys spread out, tucking themselves away for a tiny bit of privacy.

"This is ridiculous," Becky grumbled. "You warned me this would be primitive camping."

"Eh, don't worry about it. Everyone else is thankful you begged. Look, even some of the tribesmen are tucked behind a tree."

"I'm not going to *look!*" Becky hissed. "They better not be looking at me, either."

"I'm standing in between you and them with a death glare," Nicholas said. "Just finish up. I need to go too."

When they were all safely back on the trail, Becky handed around her hand sanitizer, and they all seemed grateful for that as well.

"Ba'ax le je'ela'?" One of the warriors grabbed the hand sanitizer bottle and sniffed, then pulled back with a wrinkled nose. He shoved it back into Becky's hands.

"It's hand sanitizer," Levi said, rubbing his hands together. "To clean your hands. Cho'oik k'aboob."

The man shook his head and stepped back with his fellow tribesmen.

Before continuing, the team members helped each other reach into their bags for protein bars. Nicholas grabbed a handful of them out of Levi's pack and handed them to Levi. "Offer some to the men and the girl." Nicholas made a show of opening the wrapper and taking a bite to show them what the little bars were for.

"Lela' jaanal," Levi said, offering the food. Most of the men stayed in their positions, but the curious man stepped forward again. He sniffed the bar and took a bite. Then he turned his head and spit the bite onto the ground behind him.

"Ma' bin jaanal." He shook his head and handed the bar to the chief's daughter. She sniffed the protein bar, wrinkled her nose, and handed the bar to Levi.

Levi wrapped the bar and gave it to Nicholas. "Will you put this back in my bag? They say it's not food." Levi chuckled and took a bite of the one he already had open.

The tribal chief's daughter pulled aside one of the warriors and spoke quietly to him in their native tongue. He then took off running ahead.

"What did she say?" Nicholas asked.

"I think she told him that their guests were hungry and that he should run ahead to have the tribe prepare a meal for us." Levi bowed his head to the woman in thanks and spoke softly. "Níib óolal."

She grunted and flipped her braid as she turned to keep leading the march.

"Feisty little thing," Levi muttered under his breath and Nicholas chuckled.

"Hope she's not already married." Nicholas pushed his brother's shoulder playfully.

"Shut up." Levi bit his lips, but a smile showed in his eyes.

If Nicholas thought a beautiful professor was out of his league, Levi had an uphill battle crushing on a Mayan princess.

Chapter Sixteen

Tiani Sayid

After another forty-five minutes of walking parallel to the mounds along an actual path created by the Mayan tribe, they were led into a small tent village not much bigger than the campsites the foresters had created for the team.

The tribe seemed to use similar camouflaging techniques by only clearing as many trees as necessary, leaving the canopy intact. This site didn't look permanent or that it had been occupied for long. The trees were freshly cut.

Nicholas smelled the food and almost sighed with relief. The quickly lowering sun was a concern if they were going to have shelter before night and that was the most important issue, he reminded Levi. "Ask them if we can set up our tents."

"Je'el u páajtal k instalar k koonolo'ob ba'atelilo'?" Levi asked the tribal chief's daughter, then pointed to the sun going down. "Ma'ili' ti' u ponga le k'iino'."

"Mi je'ele'." She held up a hand, indicating the team should stay right there and wait for her. Then she lifted her chin and headed straight for the largest tent.

Nicholas reached for Becky's hand and pulled her close, wishing he could promise everything would be okay, but knowing he couldn't make such promises.

After a few minutes, the chief's daughter emerged, holding open the tent flap for a large man wearing a similar headdress as his daughter, but much larger. His bare chest and arms were tattooed and muscular.

All the team members straightened their stance, and the warriors stood at attention.

His daughter spoke privately to her father and pointed at their group. Levi took one step forward, and the warriors moved in on them.

"Venimos tu Jets' óolal," Levi called out to the tribal leader. "Je'el u béeytal k p'áatal ta wéetel le áak'aba'? I asked them if we could stay here tonight and told them we come in peace."

"Ba'ax a k'áat?" the tribal leader called back. That question seemed to come up a lot this evening. Everyone wanted to know what the others intended.

"We want to sleep here and talk," Levi said, then translated. "Táak k weenel waye' ka t'aan."

"Untie my tent from my backpack," Nicholas said, turning his back to Levi. "Show them we have shelter."

Levi quickly did as his brother suggested and held up the tent for the tribe to see. "Yaan k tu'ux u yookoj maaki'."

The tribal leader crossed the small clearing and stood before Levi, reaching out to touch the sturdy canvas.

"Je'el u páajtal k ts'áik k koonolo'ob Ma'ili' ti' u ponga le k'iino'?" Levi asked. "Can we set up our tents before the sun sets?" He pointed to the sun again.

The leader nodded once and took a step back, retreating to stand beside his daughter. The warriors barely relaxed their offensive stance while the team's site manager, Jonas, started barking out orders.

"Set up your tents similar to how you would have if we were at the prepared campsite," Jonas said. "Act natural as if this is no big deal. So far, they haven't been hostile. Let's keep it that way."

With very little further communication, the team of exhausted archaeologists set to work preparing their tents in the waning light. As each completed their own tents, they helped each other so that everyone would finish as quickly as possible.

Levi was one of the first to return to the tribal leader and his daughter, allowing Nicholas and Becky to finish setting up his tent. Even from this distance, Nicholas could hear their conversation but didn't understand a word.

Gradually the team members returned to the clearing and stood close to the campfire, where they were given small bowls of meat stew with vegetables and herbs drenched in a heavenly gravy.

Nicholas bypassed the food temporarily and took his place at his brother's side, still holding Becky's hand. Timothy, the excavation director, also joined them.

Levi began introductions and told the leaders each of their names. Then he turned to his team. "My friends, may I present Chief Gabor Sayid and his daughter, Tiani Sayid."

"Sayid?" Nicholas asked. "Are they related to the princes of Madain Saleh?" Nicholas had heard the stories of their uncle's best friends who had once been heralded as princes in some Middle Eastern nation that no longer existed.

"Marcos Sayid leti'e' ka'ach in bisabuelo." The chief lifted his chin with pride.

"Prince Marcos was his great-grandfather," Levi said with creased brows and a suspicious undertone to his words. "But that doesn't make sense. He's too old."

"Not if he's referring to Prince Marcos's grandfather," Nicholas said. "Benjamin's father."

"I thought Benjamin was an only child," Levi mumbled.

"Apparently there are more branches of the Sayid family tree than we realized," Nicholas answered his twin. "What an interesting twist to this already confusing day."

Chapter Seventeen

Final Will and Testament

W ithout seeking direction from her father, Tiani hurried away and returned from her tent, holding an envelope, which she handed to Levi. "Je'ela wáaj u páajtal a xook le ba'ala'?"

"She wants to know if I can read this," Levi said, taking the envelope. Nicholas and Timothy both peered over Levi's shoulder.

"It's in Spanish," Timothy said. "Most of us should be able to read Spanish."

"I wonder if she can read the letter." Levi looked up at her. "Je'ela wáaj u páajtal a xook le ba'ala'?"

"Ma'." Tiani shook her head.

"Can you *speak* Spanish?" Levi chuckled, probably realizing he needed to ask her in Yucatec. "Ba'ax je'el u páajtal a t'aan kastláan t'aan?"

"Si, puedo hablar español," Tiani answered in perfect Spanish.

"She speaks Spanish," Levi called out to the group with a giant smile on his face. "I wonder if all of them speak Spanish. Ba'ax je'el u páajtal a t'aan kastláan t'aan?" He waved his hand around, pointing to the warriors and the tribal chief.

Tiani again answered in the affirmative, explaining they spoke Spanish when they traded with the local villages.

For the rest of the evening, most everyone conversed in a broken combination of Spanish, Yucatec, and English. Nicholas sensed the team and the tribe relax into the common language with a mutual gratitude to understand one another without the need for a translator.

Eventually they circled back to the strange letter that Tiani had handed Levi. He read aloud to the group in Spanish, then read it again, translating into English to offer clarification for those in the group who were only mildly fluent in Spanish.

"This is a final will and testament," Levi explained. "I, Prince Marcos Sayid of Mada'in Saleh, do hereby bequeath my blessing to my wife, Akna Sayid, and our son, Emir Sayid, along with twenty-three million Mexican pesos, to be held in perpetuity until at which time they should wish to draw from the account."

"Your little Mayan princess is a millionaire," Nicholas mumbled. "Probably several times over if it's been gathering interest for three generations."

"There's also information here about the local bank where the funds are being held," Levi said. "The account is in Flores."

Nicholas felt compelled to offer a formal greeting to the princess and tell her he was honored to meet her. "Princesa Tiani, me siento honrado de conocerte."

Other members of the team also bowed their heads in respect. There were murmurs among the tribesmen. Her elevated status was news to them as well.

"Su Alteza"—Nicholas bowed to the tribal chief addressing him as Your Highness—"Me siento honrado de conocerte." Nicholas wanted to make the message clear. The American scientists held the Mayan royal family in high esteem. This turn of events could actually go a long way to improving relations between the two groups.

They would use this to their advantage.

Chapter Eighteen

Temporary Settlement

How Prince Marcos had become associated with the tribe was a mystery not fully solved. From what Tiani and Chief Gabor could piece together with Nicholas and Levi, Prince Marcos must have traveled to Tikal sometime after the death of his first wife, Lyla, and met Akna at one of the village trading posts, fell in love, and married. They had a son, Emir, and stayed married for the remainder of their lives.

But Akna refused to leave her tribe, and Marcos refused to leave the luxuries of the modern world and his commitment and duties as Crown Prince of Madain Saleh to live in the wilderness. He traveled to visit his wife frequently and left her with over a million dollars when he died, but none of the tribe could read or write so the will was meaningless to them. The fact that they still had the will was a miracle in itself.

Akna and Emir must have understood its importance and impressed upon Emir's son, Eadrich the necessity of holding onto that envelope, and that importance was passed on to Gabor, who shared the envelope with Tiani.

The envelope came with a legend about a light-skinned people who would come with complicated gadgets so futuristic the people bringing them would seem like gods. In reality, most of what the team of scientists had was basic survival materials: satellite phones, computers, prepackaged food and water, high-end shelters. Other than the LiDAR technology, everything else was equipment the Americans, Mexicans, and Guatemalans took for granted as commonplace.

After a full day of trekking through the dense jungle, followed by hours of being marched at the point of a spear, followed by hours of trying to understand one another, none of them could keep their eyes opened.

Thankfully the tents were already in place and people began retiring to their respective places of refuge.

There was an unspoken understanding that the following day would be a day of rest and regrouping, trying to figure out where to go from here. The tribe members still didn't understand what the team of scientists were doing there and why they wanted to see the temple pyramid. Somehow the team needed to explain the modern technology, the importance of preserving the inscriptions, and to convince them to show the team the rest of the way to the temple now that they were completely off track.

Explaining the team's desire to study the temple pyramid proved to be more of a challenge than they anticipated. Modern technology included concepts that exceeded the tribal members' limited understanding. They were warriors, protectors, watchmen, but not scientists. The only experience they'd had with antiquities was that of looters, thieves, destroyers. And they only learned of those through trade with the local villagers.

As far as their trade partners were concerned, the tribe was a small group of nomads who lived in the jungle, subsisting on limited resources. By trading in a variety of locations on opposite sides of the jungle, they were able to conceal their vast population.

For hundreds of years, looters had yet to discover the existence of this most sacred ancient site. Generations of this tribe had fiercely guarded its location. Because of the spiral of mounds surrounding the central pyramid, anyone wishing to search the area gave up after experiencing a maze of hills and valleys, dense jungle without paths, and no obvious ruins in this wilderness.

Looters were correct in that respect. There were no ruins in this part of the wilderness, save this one location in the center of a complex spiral of hidden trails.

The path they had traveled that evening had been newly created in response to the foresters' invasion in recent weeks. The tribe seemed to inherently understand that the small clearings were intended to be used by someone for a temporary settlement, but they didn't know for who or for what reason. Upon discovering the clearings, the tribe had created their own temporary settlement and lay in wait for the looters, ready to ambush them.

Levi's ability to communicate in their native tongue had confused them. Most local looters would have spoken Spanish and been far more savage in appearance and stature.

Nicholas thanked his twin for diligently studying his chosen field of linguistics and said goodnight. He collapsed into his bedroll, pulled Becky into his arms, and fell asleep almost immediately.

Chapter Nineteen

Happy Wife, Happy Life

Nicholas hadn't intended to get married that day.

After sleeping late into the morning, the team was welcomed to the campfires of the Mayan tribe members with promises of a hot breakfast served with hesitation and suspicion.

The strides gained toward building relationships the previous evening had waned in the daylight as the tribesmen still couldn't grasp the purpose of the scientists' invasion of their jungle nor their interest in the sacred temple pyramid.

Rather than leading the team of scientists to the pyramid, the chief decided to bring them to his village. He reasoned they could take the time required to understand one another, eat real food, replenish their dwindling water supply from the tribe's hidden cenote, and rest. The village was also significantly closer to the temple pyramid and involved an actual path rather than needing to chop through the jungle with machetes. The team could hardly argue.

So, they packed up their tents just as they'd done the previous morning and followed the chief and tribe members without much choice. They weren't quite being led at the tips of the warriors' spears, but they were followed closely by tribesmen on all sides.

The walk wasn't long, and by mid-day, they entered a surprisingly large village with thatched roofs made of palm leaves and low rock walls along paths of earth. Dwellings were small and spread out across a large region to avoid the need to disrupt the tree canopy, keeping them hidden from airplanes. The village was so well-hidden that the LiDAR scans had barely picked it up as man-made. The remote sensing analysts had dismissed the blip as outlying antiquities near the main temple pyramid.

To describe the village as off the grid was an understatement. The tribe subsisted off the land, growing their own food and utilizing the jungle forests as their natural gardens. They had a few animals and, in honor of their guests, had slaughtered a large calf and were in the process of preparing a meal for the entire village. There would be a celebration that evening.

Upon arriving in the village, the scientists set up their tents in the locations they were shown and treated the site as they would have any other campsite along their way.

They were taken to a small cenote of crystal-clear water and were instructed to refill their water jugs. The tribal members drank water directly from the sinkhole of groundwater, declaring that it was perfectly safe. Knowing the likelihood of microorganisms to which the scientists have zero immunities, they chose to purify their drinking water prior to consumption.

The afternoon was spent introducing the team to the village and touring the many structures, most of which were small homes crowded with many children.

The chief was fascinated by Nicholas and Levi, wondering how they could be the same person living in two bodies. He had no concept of twins. He also wondered how the men shared one wife.

Levi stepped away and shook his head, explaining he was not part of Nicholas and Becky's relationship.

Nicholas explained that he loved Becky but that she was his girlfriend not his wife. That upset the chief. He was insistent that no one should sleep together until they were married. Although Nicholas and Becky both agreed with the concept in principle, there wasn't much they could do about the challenge until they returned home to America. Married or not, he wasn't letting Becky sleep alone in the jungle.

"Yaan u ts'o'okol beelo'." The chief pointed to himself and nodded his head definitively. "Le áak'aba'."

"Uh… I think he said he would perform the wedding." Levi chuckled nervously. "Tonight."

"Very funny," Nicholas said. "We'll get married when we get home to America."

"K'a'anan ts'o'okol u bey ma' weenel múuch' le áak'aba'." The chief looked angry.

"He says you need to be married before you sleep together tonight," Levi said.

"Humor him," Becky said out of the side of her mouth. "It's not like it's for real. We can still have a wedding when we get back to the States."

"Are you sure?" Nicholas asked, just as quietly. "Don't you want a white dress and cake and dancing and your father to walk you down the aisle?"

"Sure, but if performing some traditional Mayan ritual will make him happy, what the heck?" Becky said. "We need him to help us get to the temple pyramid. What could it hurt?"

"If you insist," Nicholas said. "You know what they say, happy wife, happy life."

Becky giggled and stepped closer to the chief, bowing her head in respect. She didn't know how to say yes or thank you in Yucatec, but she could answer in Spanish. "Si, gracias."

The chief nodded his approval and said something to his daughter, waving her over. Tiani seemed surprised and looked them up and down with a creased brow.

Levi translated what he'd said and spoke directly to Becky. "The chief wants Tiani to help you get ready for your wedding. You're supposed to follow her."

"Uh... okay." Becky squeezed Nicholas's hand and stepped away from him, then glanced behind and offered Nicholas a nervous wave. "See ya at the altar."

Chapter Twenty

Shaman's Blessing

"He's going to say everything in Yucatec so I'll just translate on the fly," Levi said. They were standing together in the middle of the little village near the chief, waiting for Becky to return from Tiani's bridal makeover. "Just think of the whole thing as if it's a shaman's blessing."

"I'm not worried about it, man," Nicholas said. "If this makes him happy, and Becky's happy, I'll go along with it. You might want to pay close attention to the ceremony though, because it's going to be identical to yours in a few months when you marry your Princess Tiani." Surrounding them stood half the tribe and the entire team of archaeologists. No pressure.

"Think about it. Between the two of them, we're combining everything we ever thought we wanted in a wife," Levi said.

"Speaking of which." Nicholas tapped his twin's shoulder, and they turned in the direction of the largest hut in the village where Tiani emerged with a triumphant smirk, as if she personally had transformed Becky into a bride.

Becky walked out with her hand through the arm of Dr. Timothy Cathcart, her boss, and their excavation director. Nicholas almost laughed out loud at the fitting substitute for Becky's father. He kept reminding himself this wasn't real.

That colorful tribal gown Tiani had loaned her was not the elegant white dress he'd imagined. The ring of flowers placed as a crown on her head was not what she would have chosen. Still, she looked beautiful, and he was honored to be marrying her, however strange the whole situation felt.

The tribal chief slash prince slash shaman welcomed the ladies to stand with him, and Becky took Nicholas's hand, facing him the way the chief directed. A tribal member stepped forward and startled them by blowing into a large conch shell like a horn.

As the chief spoke in Yucatec, Levi translated, and the words were very sweet and down-to-earth, literally, calling upon mother earth and the sky and the elements of nature. He asked permission from the four cardinal points, handed Nicholas and Becky each a seed, and explained that the seed represented the starting of their new life together. He blessed them with abundance, love, and positive intentions. He explained that when they cast the seeds upon the land and into the water, they would get what they wish for in their relationship.

This didn't seem like a wedding, more like a shaman's blessing, as Levi had mentioned. The ceremony ended with women from the tribe bringing rose petals and tossing them over Nicholas and Becky as a way of dropping positive intentions.

The entire ceremony involved burning incense, and beating on drums, and blowing conch shells, and eventually morphed into a celebration where everyone was dancing and smiling and laughing.

Nicholas could envision his twin brother embracing this celebration as the perfect wedding, but Nicholas vowed to provide Becky with a white dress and cake and her parents and friends and family in attendance. They might be married in the eyes of the tribal chief, but Nicholas was going to watch his bride walk down an aisle on the arm of her father. Someday.

Entering the tent they'd shared the first two nights felt strange. Now that the chief had declared them married, there was this unspoken expectation that tonight they would magically flip a switch from not having sex to having sex. But the reality was not as straightforward.

Nicholas sat on the bedroll and met Becky's eyes with apprehension. He cleared his throat. "That wasn't exactly how I'd pictured our... wedding."

"Me neither." Becky bit her lower lip, brow furrowed and a tension in her shoulders that was visible from where Nicholas sat two feet away.

"This doesn't feel right." Nicholas lowered his gaze and fiddled with the sleeping bag he was sitting on.

Becky let out a breath that sounded like relief. "I agree."

"You do?" Nicholas lifted his gaze again, feeling hope. "I was afraid you'd be disappointed if we didn't..."

"Have sex tonight?" Becky finished his sentence.

"Yeah."

"I was afraid *you* would be disappointed," Becky said. "I mean, I haven't showered in, like, four days, we have zero privacy, and I kind of have this romanticized vision of taking our time and getting to know each other's bodies and, and... making love to each other, not just having sex because we're supposed to have sex on our wedding night."

"I agree one hundred percent." Nicholas opened his arms and reached for Becky. She came to sit on his lap and snuggled into his arms. They both sighed simultaneously. "As hungry as I've been for you, I am seriously content to just hold you in my arms tonight."

"Me too," she whispered.

"Let's take this marriage thing slowly, at our own pace," Nicholas said. He pulled back a little and looked down at her. "I love you so much, and I've loved getting to know you these past few months since you showed up on my doorstep. When I make love to you for the first time, I want that experience to feel right and to be on our terms."

"Thank you," Becky said. "For understanding. For loving me. For being the kind of man I'm proud to call my husband."

"I like the sound of that." Nicholas leaned forward and kissed Becky as she reached for him, wrapping her arms around his neck and shoulders.

Nicholas laid her down on their bedroll and kissed her more passionately than they probably should have when they'd just stated definitively that they weren't ready to have sex yet. He found himself very content with just that, and his body surprisingly agreed.

Eventually they fell asleep in each other's arms, relaxed and happy, all pressure gone, the weight on their shoulders lifted, able to merely *be* together.

Chapter Twenty-One

Cenote

By some stroke of luck, none of the team members, or tribal members, paid them any attention the following morning. There was no teasing or taunting or innuendoes. Everyone knew the day was set aside for planning and preparing and resting. Some people weren't even awake or out of their tents when Nicholas emerged.

For the second day in a row, the team was treated to a full hot breakfast, complete with corn bread, tortillas, eggs, and some sort of sausage similar to chorizo but with a slightly different flavoring. If there wasn't still an underlying urgency to begin research at the temple pyramid, they might be tempted to stay in this beautiful village forever. Maybe not during the rainy season though.

After the mid-day meal, Tiani approached Levi and spoke to him briefly, then pointed over in a westerly direction. The two of them walked over to Timothy where he stood together with some of the team members, including the field guide and site manager.

Timothy was preparing to fly the drone up and over the last mound to get the lay of the terrain. He had already used the satellite phone to call the support team who would be dropping off supplies at the final destination and gave them the full explanation of this turn of events.

The ability to communicate with someone in a different location was foreign to the tribal members. When Timothy had brought out the drone, many of the brave warriors had cowered to the ground in fear of the strange magic flying spider.

Nicholas was curious enough about his brother's conversation to head in that direction and eavesdrop. Tiani was telling them something about a slightly larger cenote nearby that the tribe used as a bathing area. That caught Nicholas's full attention. There were many of these sinkholes in the region, some very large and famous. Others, apparently quite well hidden. Some seemed bottomless and boundless caverns traveling miles underground with sparkling clear water and mysterious caves. Others, tiny like a pond. Tiani said they had a special biodegradable soap that was safe for the delicate ecosystem of the cenotes.

As Becky had mentioned the previous evening, they'd gone four days without running water and thus without proper hygiene. They had expected to be settled at their more permanent campsite by now. Once there, the drop team would send them the equipment to build a makeshift shower. A well had already been dug. A bath in a cenote sounded like heaven in comparison.

Word spread quickly that later in the day they would have a chance to bathe, and spirits were lifted by the mere thought. Several of the guys jockeyed to go first, but Nicholas held back, a plan developing in his mind. He turned to Becky.

"You and I should go last," he whispered.

"Like, together?" Becky raised her eyebrows.

"Sure, why not? We're married now, right? If you're not comfortable with the idea, I'm totally fine. Or if, maybe you'd like to keep swimsuits on and just think of it as going swimming in a pond together."

"I think I could handle going swimming together." She still sounded hesitant, but Nicholas was willing to give her space and time to get used to the idea. "I *could* use some help washing my hair."

"I would *love* to help you wash that incredible mane of yours." He stepped closer and wrapped his arms around her waist.

"You did suggest I wear my hair down at our wedding." She rested her hands on his forearms and glanced up at him with a demure flirt in her eyes.

"We're just drawing out our wedding over the course of several days." He leaned down and kissed her lightly, looking forward to that evening.

After a hearty meal of homemade stew and corn bread, guys began trickling down to be the first to bathe. They returned with wet hair wearing clean clothes and euphoric expressions. Nicholas got more and more excited and nervous as the numbers dwindled.

Levi was one of the last to bathe and when he handed off the soap, he winked and said, "Take all the time you want, and I'll have a surprise for you when you emerge from the cenote."

"What surprise?" Nicholas called after him, talking to his retreating back.

"You'll see," Levi called over his shoulder. "Have fun."

Nicholas turned to Becky. "You ready?"

She had already changed into her swimsuit, which she wore under a modest cover up.

"Where did you get this?" He fingered the material, a woven cloth similar to what the tribal women wore.

"Tiani loaned it to me." Becky twirled as if showing off an exclusive gown on the runway of a fashion show.

"It's beautiful." He held out his hand to lead her toward the sinkhole. "Come on, let's go for a swim."

A limestone cavern had been partially exposed by a collapsed portion of rock to form a little cavern of cool water so natural and clear they could see the bottom even in the near-darkness that had already crept upon them. A sliver of sunlight angled in such a way as to make the cavern almost glow. The tribal members likely knew this when suggesting the time and location to the team of scientists.

Nicholas removed his T-shirt and sandals but left on his swim trunks, as promised. When Becky slipped off her modest cover up, his breath caught, and his jaw dropped. She was an elegant lady while wearing business attire, relaxed and casual in a science lab, and an outdoorsman while on the trek. But in a swimsuit, Becky was voluptuous. Nicholas had been taught to be a gentleman and not ogle women, but having her as his wife meant he had permission to appreciate every curve of her beautiful body.

Lifting his jaw off the ground, Nicholas held out a hand to assist Becky down the short staircase into the glowing pool. The cylindrical sides formed vertical walls that dropped off quickly into an area not quite up to his chest but almost to Becky's shoulders. His disappointment at concealing her body was assuaged by the knowledge that he was allowed the honor of helping wash her hair.

Never had anything in his life felt so provocative as weaving the all-natural soap Tiani gave them up and around and into Becky's hair, taking his time and relishing the opportunity, rinsing and rewashing. When he'd done as good of a job as he could do in a jungle sinkhole, she asked if she could wash his hair. That required Nicholas to crouch down for her to reach his head. It would have taken him less than a minute to wash what little hair he had, but she made the experience last several minutes. He moaned in pleasure at the feeling of having her hands massaging his scalp.

When his hair was finally rinsed, Nicholas didn't want to wait any longer and turned around, pulling Becky close and crushing his lips to hers, hungry with desire. She matched his hunger with a near frenzy of passion. Slowing his kisses, he boldly reached to untie her bikini top and tossed the tiny article of clothing onto the bank near the stairs.

Neither of them needed a roadmap to explore every hill and valley on each other's bodies. Neither of them suggested an end to their swim, if that was still an accurate description of the experience. Neither of them wanted to stop, nor did they.

Eventually the remaining parts of their swimsuits rested on the bank and nothing stood in their way.

As he'd predicted over and over the past few months, everything about that night was worth waiting for. Everything about Becky was worth waiting for. Everything about marriage was worth waiting for.

"We need to get to our tent," Becky whispered. "We're nearly out of daylight, and this cavern will be pitch black soon."

They helped each other up the stairs, gathered discarded articles of clothing and wrapped themselves in towels. They hoped to sneak into the camp and slip into their tent unnoticed, avoiding the need to don clothing just to remove them again. When they came around the corner past the screen of trees and shrubs, they found Levi's surprise.

Their tent had been moved and placed within twenty feet of the cenote where they'd spent the past hour. One flap had been tied open, revealing a display of tiny flashlights arranged like romantic candles. A note rested on the bedroll in Levi's handwriting.

Congratulations on your recent nuptials. Enjoy an evening of privacy and relaxation. Signed, Your Excavation Team

"Well, gosh, don't have to ask me twice." Nicholas held out his arms to welcome his new bride into what quickly became the best night of their lives.

Chapter Twenty-Two

Have a Fun Trek

"D r. Stephenson and Dr. Benson," Levi called from outside their tent. "Are the two of you planning to wake up anytime soon?"

"No," Nicholas and Becky mumbled simultaneously. He hadn't realized she was awake. His chuckle and her giggle did funny things to his skin where they connected. Their legs and arms and bodies were still intertwined even in sleep.

He wouldn't have thought there was any stamina left, yet here he was again filled with desire and longing. Ignoring his twin brother, Nicholas moaned softly and pulled his wife close again, connecting their lips in another passionate kiss.

"I'm still standing right here." Levi cleared his throat from outside their tent.

"Uninvited." Nicholas barely pulled his mouth away from Becky's long enough to answer.

"We need to get packed up and trek over the last mound today," Levi said.

"Not interested," Nicholas mumbled, moving his kisses to Becky's throat and under her ears. She arched her back and let out a soft whimper.

"Have you forgotten we are here in Guatemala for an archeological excavation, not a honeymoon?" Levi asked. "We kinda need our archeologist for that."

"For what?" Nicholas asked, finally lifting his head. "We're not actually conducting a dig. All we need is our linguist, and that's you. So, go away."

"I'm not allowed to go away without dragging the two of you with me, so please get dressed."

Nicholas laughed so suddenly it came out as a snort, which made Becky giggle again. "Not a chance in Hades I'm getting dressed right this minute."

"You're gonna get all three of us fired." Levi was grasping at straws now.

"We're billionaires volunteering our time and backdoor funding most of the expedition. Plus, I'm the top environmental archaeologist in my field, Becky's highly valued at her university, and you are the only linguist fluent in every ancient and modern Mayan language in the world. The chances of them firing any of us is ludicrous, so please go away."

"You're funding the expedition?" There was awe in Becky's voice and a sparkle in her eyes.

"I'll tell you all about it sometime." He leaned closer and kissed the tip of her nose. "When we're not... distracted."

"Do I need to remind you that you'll be in breach of contract if you get Dr. Benson pregnant?" Levi brought up Timothy's jest from the first day of introductions. "You might want to stop having sex for a couple of days to lessen the likelihood of that happening."

"Ha! That's the funniest thing you've said all day," Nicholas said.

"It's okay, Dr. Stephenson," Becky called out to Levi. "You can tell Dr. Cathcart that I'm on the pill, and I promise not to get pregnant for another couple of years."

"You are?" Nicholas couldn't hide a grin, wondering how long in advance she'd been planning this getaway.

"Yeah, hormone regulation when I had ovarian cysts in my early twenties."

"Ah, and here I was hoping it was in anticipation of marrying me," Nicholas said.

"We can pretend that's the reason if you want," Becky said with a sly grin.

"I want." Nicholas didn't elaborate on what he wanted, just pressed his lips to hers in another passionate kiss.

"Ugh, I'm outta here." Levi faked gagging and started to walk away.

Nicholas pulled back from their kiss long enough to call out, "It's about time." Then he felt bad for dismissing his twin so casually. "Hey, man, have a fun trek. See ya in a couple of days."

"Maybe," Becky said. "If I let you out of my arms long enough."

"I have no desire to be out of your arms," Nicholas mumbled.

Her answering kiss silenced any further discussion.

Chapter Twenty-Three

Life Altering

"Tiani, how long does it take to walk from here to the temple pyramid?" Nicholas asked. When she shook her head in confusion, at first Nicholas questioned whether she was willing to show him the way. Then he remembered she didn't speak English. He translated to Spanish and tried again. "¿Cuánto tiempo se tarda en caminar desde aquí hasta el templo?"

"Veinte minutos," she said with a shrug.

"Twenty minutes?" Nicholas gaped at her. "To get over that mound? ¿Para superar ese montículo?"

She scoffed. "Nosotras no caminamos sobre el montículo." She shook her head and rolled her eyes.

"You don't walk over the mound?" Nicholas laughed. "How do you get to the temple? ¿Cómo se llega al templo?"

"A través del túnel." Her statement was so matter of fact as if the answer was obvious.

"A tunnel?"

"Si." She nodded with a smirk.

With excitement, Becky asked Tiani if she would show them the way. "¿Nos mostrarás el camino?"

"¿Ahora mismo?"

"Si, right now, ahora mismo." Nicholas responded.

Tiani started to walk away, but Nicholas stopped her to ask if they could leave their tent here in the village.

"¿Podemos dejar nuestra carpa aquí?" Nicholas pointed over to where he and Becky still had their tent set up, where it had been for two days, near the cenote.

She nodded and then gestured for them to follow her. "Vamonos."

Nicholas took Becky's hand and followed the Mayan princess toward the mound and a little to the west, where she ducked between several trees and held aside the branches of some bushes to reveal an ancient earthen tunnel that was as fascinating as it was terrifying.

Holding out the flashlight, Nicholas revealed a dark hole the other side of which could not be seen from where they stood. He turned to Tiani, asking if she would come with them.

"¿Vendrás con nosotros?" Nicholas raised his eyebrows in question, nervous to enter this void without a practiced guide.

"Un momento por favor." Tiani held up her hand and asked them to wait a moment. She returned with a lantern and led the way into the tunnel, Nicholas and Becky in tow.

The darkness swallowed them almost immediately, and they walked in the small space of light created by Tiani's lantern and Nicholas's flashlight. A moist, earthy smell enveloped them. The floor was smooth and hard from hundreds of years of Mayans passing through the mound to reach the temple pyramid quickly and easily. The sides and ceiling curved above them, barely higher than Nicholas's head. He tried not to think about how many pounds of gravel surrounded them. If the tunnel collapsed, they would be killed or trapped indefinitely, especially since they were the only three people who knew they were in the tunnel.

After what felt like forever, but was probably only fifteen minutes, the tunnel lightened ahead and grew brighter the closer to the end they walked. Nicholas felt the urge to run ahead and burst through the trees and brush, but stayed behind Tiani, letting her take the lead.

When they reached the end, Tiani pushed aside a camouflage similar to the one at the other end of the tunnel, and suddenly they were blinded by sunlight. Even through the shielding canopy, the sun was too strong after being in the tunnel.

Ten scientists, including his twin brother, stared with wide eyes and gaping mouths while Nicholas and Becky shielded their eyes. As with most everything, Tiani seemed to take the intrusive sun with stride and barely showed an annoyance.

"Where the heck did you come from?" Levi asked the question all of them were probably thinking.

"There's a tunnel." Nicholas pointed behind him as if the evidence wasn't immediately in front of their eyes. "Took us less than twenty minutes."

Several of the guys glanced up the hill of the mound, the one they wasted an entire day of travel chopping through with machetes when they could have walked casually through a tunnel.

As his team of scientists gawked at the hidden tunnel, Nicholas stepped forward, finally seeing the temple pyramid for the first time. Although camouflaged beneath overgrowth and shaded by the jungle trees, the structure was enormous.

"Oh my gosh." He was at a loss for words after that. In all his years studying archaeology, crisscrossing the globe to excavate digs that were tiny in comparison, Nicholas had never encountered anything like this. No amount of research prepared him for this.

This Mayan temple was life-altering.

Chapter Twenty-Four

The Whole Story

"You have to come see this," Levi said, grabbing Nicholas's hand and pulling him gently around the side of the temple pyramid. "The pictures don't do it justice."

Levi was right. The majesty of the ancient building couldn't be captured digitally. It had to be experienced.

Nicholas had to watch his feet on the uneven ground, careful not to trip over roots. He remembered Becky following behind him and glanced back to smile. She was just as enthralled. He didn't bother reaching for her hand. They both needed to experience this for themselves.

They made their way around the corner of the temple pyramid where the team had more fully cleared the ground in order to step closer to the walls for a better close-up experience.

"So, it *is* more detailed than Stella 5 from Izapa." Nicholas could feel his heart racing. "That wasn't just our fantastical idea based on excitement."

"The whole thing reads like a codex," Levi said, hurrying ahead. "The same geometric and hieroglyphic narrative as the Egyptian system from the twenty-sixth dynasty. The same measurements based on the Egyptian cubit, and the same radius of the circle of the Babylonian cubit. And get this; there are 260 of them."

"To mark the calendar circuit for the sun's 260 days southern passage," Nicholas guessed.

"Or to mark the 260-day cycle that represents the gestation period celebrating the creation of man," Levi corrected.

"You're always looking for a religious angle, aren't you?" Nicholas rolled his eyes. "You can't just see the symbolism as worshiping the sun?"

"In Izapa, yes," Levi said. "The entire Izapa plaza is laid out to highlight the passage of the sun overhead, warranting the designation as a temple to the sun. The Izapa sequence is dedicated to the four seasons and the lunar months."

"The Mayan were smart," Nicholas said.

"They still are." Levi glanced back at Tiani, who stood regally, her chin lifted with a serene boredom that came from not understanding a word they were staying. Levi translated his comment for her alone. "Le maaya'obo' ku inteligentes."

A tiny smile played at the corner of Tiani's mouth, and then she pulled her face back into her stoic facade.

"Anyway, the complexity is on the same level as Stella 5," Levi said, returning to the task at hand. "But Izapa only shows a rendering of the tree of life, which is one tiny portion of the story. This is like having 260 stelae side by side wrapping around the entire base of the temple pyramid, and it tells the *whole* story."

"What do you mean by the whole story?" Becky asked, stepping closer and fingering the ornate carvings.

"Back to the creation of man." Levi's whisper was almost reverent, and he raised his eyebrows. "You ask me how I can connect a religious angle. How can I not?"

Nicholas felt chills run up his spine. He'd heard Levi's argument before. If all ancient texts from opposite sides of the world told the same story... maybe the story was true.

Chapter Twenty-Five

Closer than Your Twin

"**W**as it as good as you thought it would be?" Levi asked.

Nicholas found himself alone with his twin brother for the first time since marrying Becky. He knew exactly what Levi was asking. He glanced over his shoulder to see if anyone was close enough to overhear.

After Levi had explained the translations in very basic detail to his captive audience, the team members gradually fell back to begin preparation for the mid-day meal.

Becky excused herself when she was called away by her boss, Timothy, and left Nicholas with a quick kiss that held the promise of more later.

"Way better. Anyone who has ever used the phrase 'better than sex' to describe anything other than sex, has never had sex."

Levi tossed his head back in laughter. "I will never use that phrase again, I promise."

"No, I sincerely hope you have the opportunity to understand what I mean by that statement," Nicholas said. "This is the opposite of the phrase 'I wouldn't wish this on my worst enemy.' I *do* wish this on my best and closest friend."

"Can't get any closer or best than your twin."

"Until you marry the woman you were meant to be with for eternity. Then you realize there is someone even closer than your twin."

"I'm not sure if I should feel jealous or happy for you."

"I hope someday you have the chance to be happy for me."

"I am happy for you, man." Levi glanced to his right and Nicholas followed his gaze over to where the young graduate student, Matt, was speaking animatedly to Tiani. She politely gave him half of her attention while glancing frequently in their direction. "And I do look forward to that someday."

"You better go rescue her, or she'll spook and fly through that tunnel and never come back."

"Speaking of... where is your stuff? Are you staying in the village?"

"Do you really want us over here?" Nicholas raised his eyebrows.

"Probably not." Levi shook his head. "Still, I want to be where you are, and I want to see that tunnel."

"And spend the evening with Tiani?"

"That too, I suppose."

"Fine, pack up when you get a chance and come spend the evening with your future wife while I spend the night in the arms of my forever wife." They began walking in Tiani's direction. The relief on her face was almost comical.

"Forever, huh?" Levi spoke from the corner of his mouth. "I take it that means you're not planning to get an annulment upon returning to the States?"

"Just the opposite," Nicholas said. "We're planning a wedding."

As they approached Matt and Tiani, Nicholas bowed regally to the princess, then turned to Matt, continuing in the language he was likely speaking with Tiani to ask him where Timothy and Becky had run off to.

"¿Dónde están el Dr. Cathcart y mi esposa?"

"Over by his tent, I think," Matt said. His frustration evident in his creased brows and hard glare.

"¿Me mostraras el camino?" Nicholas asked, still speaking Spanish for Tiani's sake to request that Matt show him where he could find their excavation director.

"Si." He continued his glare and even glanced longingly at Tiani. "Discúlpame, por favor."

As Matt began to walk away, Tiani whispered to Nicholas, "Gracias."

"De nada," Nicholas whispered back before following Matt.

As they walked away, Nicholas heard his brother switch to Yucatec as he spoke to Tiani, essentially shutting out anyone else who might want to eavesdrop. Effective tactic. He wished he had a similar language to communicate with his wife.

Then Nicholas realized he did have his own personal language with Becky, but that involved the privacy of their tent and the removal of their clothes. *Later*, he thought. Hopefully not too much later.

Chapter Twenty-Six

Resignation

"D r. Cathcart, could I borrow your satellite phone?" Nicholas skipped any formalities as he slid up behind Becky and kissed her neck.

"Only if you're using the phone to call your university and tender your resignation." Timothy laughed as he handed over the lifeline that would save them in the event of an emergency.

"Close," Nicholas said, taking the phone and handing it to Becky. "Could you please call your father? I need to formally apologize to Mr. Benson for marrying his daughter before asking his permission."

"Actually it's *Dr.* Benson to you," Becky said with a chuckle, taking the phone and starting to dial his number. Then she backspaced. "Wait, he would be at his office this time of day." She resumed punching in buttons.

"Ah, what does he have his PhD in?" Nicholas asked.

Becky chuckled. "Obstetrics. He's a *real* doctor. He sees patients and everything."

"Forgive me," Nicholas teased. "I'll be sure to offer him the level of respect he deserves." He winked over at Timothy.

"Good afternoon, could I speak with Dr. Benson please?" She pushed the button for the speakerphone.

"I'm sorry, he's seeing patients right now. Could I take a message for him?"

"Actually, I'm calling from Guatemala on a satellite phone, so unless he's delivering a baby, could you please tell him his daughter needs to speak with him?"

"Satellite phone?" the receptionist asked, flustered. "Guatemala?"

Dr. Benson must have been standing close because a man's voice in the background said, "Is my daughter okay?"

He breathlessly took the phone, clunking the receiver. Nicholas could almost see him jostling around and shoving the poor receptionist out of the way.

"Rebecca? Are you okay?"

"Yes, Daddy, I'm fine." Her sweet, innocent voice while speaking to her father was such a stark contrast to the professional lady he knew. Coupled with the flirty temptress he also knew and more importantly the sensual woman who shared his bed, Nicholas wondered how many hats this girl wore. "I have someone I'd like you to meet, and then we have a request. We need your help. We're on speakerphone, and I'd like you to meet Dr. Nicholas Stephenson, the elite environmental archaeologist I met at Boston University when we were both grad students. He teaches at Harvard now."

"You called all this way to introduce me to an archaeologist?" her father asked.

"Dr. Benson, I'm honored to speak with you, sir," Nicholas said. "You're welcome to call me Nicholas. I'm calling to apologize for marrying your daughter before requesting your permission."

"You"—Dr. Benson sounded like he was either going to choke, yell, or cry— "*married* my daughter."

"Yes, sir." Nicholas gulped. "I'm very sorry, sir. Although, I'm not sorry I married her. I'm only sorry I married her without your permission."

"Daddy, we're calling Mom next, and we'd like your help arranging a wedding back in the States as soon as we return."

"If you're already married"—he sounded like he was gritting his teeth— "why do you need to have a wedding?"

Nicholas interjected. "We want to make sure it's legal in the United States, sir. Becky deserves to have a white dress and cake and pictures with her friends and family rather than wearing the wedding costume of a Mayan princess. Plus, without the tribal chief holding a spear to our chests."

"What?" Dr. Benson was sounding more agitated.

"Daddy, we just want to have a wedding, okay? And as soon as possible. Which is why we're calling. I'll have Mamma set it up for about six weeks from now, which is about when we'll return from Guatemala."

"Six weeks?"

"I know that doesn't seem like a lot of time, but Mamma can make it happen. Besides, six weeks is a lot longer to plan a wedding than the one hour we had a few days ago."

"One hour?"

"Yes, the tribal chief insisted. He didn't want us sleeping together unless we were married."

"The sentiment to which we agreed wholeheartedly," Nicholas added. "Which is why we went along with it. Best decision I ever made." Nicholas felt his shoulders soften as he searched his wife's eyes.

"Me too," Becky said, meeting his gaze with a cheesy grin.

"Alright, alright, call your mother. I need to get back to seeing patients. Some of us work as real doctors you know?"

"Yes, of course, Dr. Benson. And thank you so much, sir. I look forward to meeting you."

"Goodbye, Daddy," Becky said. "Love you!"

"Love you, too, Rebecca." With that, the phone was disconnected, and Nicholas leaned forward to kiss his wife.

Timothy made a fake gagging noise and asked when they'd be returning to the village.

"Couple more phone calls to make first," Nicholas said, already dialing the main number for his department chairman.

A pleasant woman's voice came over the line. "Department of Anthropology, this is Helen, may I help you?"

"Helen, this is Nicholas Stephenson. Is Dr. Sedwick available?"

"Of course, Dr. Stephenson," Helen said. "Just a moment." After a couple of clicks, the chairman of the department was on the line and addressed him fondly.

"Dr. Sedwick," Nicholas said, meeting Timothy's gaze. "I'm calling from Guatemala to offer my letter of resignation. I'm moving to Houston to be near my wife."

Part Two: Separate Lives

Dr. Levi Stephenson, PhD, Linguistics

A s told by Dr. Levi Stephenson, son of Frederick Stephenson, grand-son of Alexandria (Cohen) Stephenson, great-grandson of Nicholas Cohen, great-great-grandson of Levi Cohen. Ten years after the passing of King Sayid, as the story begins...

Chapter Twenty-Seven

Traditions

"Have my brother and Rebecca been tucked away in their tent the whole time we've been gone?" Levi asked Tiani in Yucatec since they were alone at the campfire. When none of the archaeology team was around, he didn't feel he had to speak Spanish or translate to English for those who had a limited vocabulary in Spanish.

As a world-renowned scientist and professor at Harvard University with a PhD in linguistics, Levi was fluent in a variety of languages, including every known ancient and modern dialect of the Mayans. He was the only person on the archaeology expedition who could communicate with Tiani in her native language, Yucatec.

Tiani laughed, one of the few times Levi had seen her let down her guard. Growing up as the daughter of Chief Gabor Sayid, and more recently learning of her royal lineage, the mysterious and exotic Mayan princess was always so serious, so professional, so regal. Her tribe held her in high esteem, and she acted the part.

Levi discreetly hid any romantic attraction to the Mayan princess for a variety of reasons, not the least of which was a fear of rejection. But the reality of their circumstances was they lived in separate worlds.

The jungles of Guatemala, where Tiani had lived in isolation her entire twenty-nine years, was so different from his modern life in the United States. Most of the conveniences Levi took for granted would be completely foreign to her.

They could never be anything more than friends.

"Your brother's behavior with his wife is very normal for married couples," Tiani said, seeming relieved to be speaking in Yucatec. Having her words translated constantly was probably annoying. "Most newly married people remain in isolation for many days. Some even leave the tribe for a time. I was surprised when Nicholas and Rebecca asked me to lead them to visit you. Whatever married people do together makes them smile, and they are happy. I do not know. I have never been married." Tiani lowered her gaze and folded her hands in her lap.

"I have never been married either," Levi said. The late evening offered a measure of relaxation not available in the daylight. He and Tiani were sitting in full view of all other members of the tribe here in the center of the village near the community fire. But the pressures of the day were off their shoulders. They could let down their guard a little. Speak freely. Speak about topics that were a little more personal. "I've never even had a girlfriend."

"What is this word? Girlfriend?" Tiani asked, creasing her brow. "Are men in your village forbidden to speak to girls?"

"That's not what I meant." It was Levi's turn to laugh. "All men are allowed to speak to all women. A girlfriend would be a woman who is also allowed to kiss and hug and hold hands with a man before marriage."

"No." Tiani lifted her facade again. "Men and women should not touch each other before they are married."

"Things are different in America, I guess." Levi placed his hand to his chest. "But I have never kissed or hugged or held hands with a woman before."

Tiani visibly relaxed with a sigh as if she was afraid Levi had defiled himself. He almost wanted to laugh but realized in Tiani's world this was serious. The rule was so strict that her father had forced Nicholas and Becky to get married before sleeping in the same tent. Levi would need to tread carefully to avoid offending Tiani or scaring her away.

"How does a person in your tribe choose who to marry?" Levi asked, suspecting he already knew the answer. Chief Gabor seemed to have a great deal of power and respect among the tribe members. Levi wouldn't be surprised to learn the chief was the one to decide.

"My father chooses who a man can marry," Tiani said. "Women are sacred, and a man needs to prove his worth before my father will allow him to marry a woman."

"That's beautiful." Levi felt a chill travel across his arms and the heat of the jungle led him to believe the goosebumps weren't caused by cool air.

He wasn't thrilled with the idea of someone else choosing whom he could marry, but he liked the idea of men needing to prove their worth.

He also liked the idea of women being sacred. This was one of the reasons he had committed to celibacy before marriage. In all the societies he'd studied, those which seemed the happiest were those who treated marriage with sanctity. The power to create life was an honor and privilege. That power should not be taken lightly.

"Why has your father never chosen a husband for you?" Levi once again suspected he knew the answer.

Tiani lifted her chin. "No man in our village has yet to prove his worth."

"Have there been any men in your life who you've *wanted* to prove their worth?" Levi was treading lightly.

Tiani hesitated and glanced to her side, then lifted her gaze again. "Not in our village."

Levi couldn't help the tiny smile that pulled on his lips. He also noticed the twitch on her lips before she pulled together her perfect facade.

"Why are you the same person as your brother?" Tiani changed the subject. Identical twins were a phenomenon this Mayan tribe had never witnessed.

Leaning forward to poke at the campfire with a long stick, Levi considered how to answer. "Our mother had two babies on the same day. Nicholas and I lived inside of her together and were born together. We still live together. Well... now that he is married, we probably won't live together anymore." Levi's heart sank when the realization fully registered in his mind.

Levi couldn't remember the last time he'd spent a night apart from Nicholas. They shared a townhouse, shared an office at Harvard University where they were both professors, and shared a tent or hotel room when they traveled on archaeology exhibitions. They'd attended the same college and graduate school, always rooming in the dorms together, and had shared a bedroom growing up even though their family estate was worth over a billion dollars and they could easily have their own rooms.

All that changed when Nicholas married Becky three days ago. Not only would they never room together again, but Levi wasn't sure he could pitch his tent within earshot of his twin. Now that he and Becky were married, they were insufferable to be around. Apparently living thirty years on this earth without having sex causes a person to feel they need to make up for lost time by not getting out of bed for days after the wedding. Go figure.

He wanted to be happy for them, but a tiny part of him was jealous.

The funny thing was Levi wasn't jealous of Becky for stealing his twin brother. He was jealous of Nicholas for having won the competition to get married first. They'd been forever competing with each other in a good-natured way. About everything from intelligence quotient—of course Levi had the higher IQ—to who could graduate college in the fewest number of semesters—they tied—to whose portfolio would be worth more when they retired.

They even competed for the privilege to drive their candy-apple-red Lamborghini Urus. Levi allowed Nicholas to win that competition. That silly car had been Nicholas's idea and his baby. Levi had no desire to drive.

But he did have the desire to get married, and he suspected the reason had less to do with competition and more to do with his growing attraction to Tiani. Now that he knew how much fun Nicholas was having with his new bride, suddenly that's all Levi could think about.

Nicholas and Levi thought they'd be bachelors forever. What woman would want to marry an identical twin who was practically joined at the hip with his brother and spent every day studying and researching and traveling on archaeology expeditions?

Dr. Rebecca Benson had swooped in and turned their lives upside down. A ghost from Nicholas's past in one of the few college classes the twins hadn't taken together, Becky had been a graduate assistant and completely out of reach. The unattainable dream Levi never realized Nicholas had. When she showed up on their doorstep after eight years apart, asking them to accompany her on a treasure hunt to Guatemala, the twins couldn't pack fast enough.

That was one competition Levi had lost before he realized they were racing. Becky only had eyes for Nicholas even though she flirted with every man who would hold still long enough. She had every scientist on their archaeology team eating out of the palm of her hand from day one of the exhibition even though they all knew she was out of their reach as well.

Nicholas and Becky getting married was as inevitable as the sunrise. They just didn't realize they'd get married in a Guatemalan jungle village by the tribal chief who had a proverbial spear to their chests.

Princess Tiani Sayid was even less attainable than Dr. Rebecca Benson had been. What Mayan princess would be tempted by a geeky professor from America? His only endearment was the ability to speak her language.

He'd captured her attention. But would he be able to capture her heart? More importantly, should he even try?

Chapter Twenty-Eight

Twin Speak

"You still here, little brother?" Nicholas asked, patting Levi on the shoulder and sitting beside him at the breakfast table. He reached to grab a tortilla, leaning across Levi with a grin.

"I wasn't planning on trekking back through that tunnel without you, *big* brother," Levi said to his twin, the guy who had been born seven minutes earlier than him. "Where's your bride? Sleeping in?"

"Nah, just getting ready for the day, using the bathroom, that kind of thing. Whatever it is women do in the morning. Can you hand me those potatoes? I'm starving. We're coming with you over to the temple pyramid today, don't worry."

"I'm not worried," Levi said. "I just didn't want to spend the night that far apart from you again. I suppose we'll have to get used to sleeping apart if you move to Houston, huh?" Levi felt his throat catch. This was ridiculous. They were almost thirty-one years old. Time to cut the umbilical cord.

"I get it," Nicholas said. "Some identical twins never live apart, even after they're married. I didn't like being that far away from you either. I'm glad you moved your tent back into the village. We will need to figure this out though, especially if you plan to move to Guatemala."

Levi nearly spit his juice out and started coughing. Nicholas patted him on the back. Levi managed to choke out, "What makes you think I'm moving to Guatemala?"

"I don't think your little princess is going to want to move to Houston with you," Nicholas said.

"Who says I'm moving to Houston?"

"Dude, you couldn't even spend two nights apart with a twenty-minute walk between us. How are you going to stay in Cambridge when I live in Houston?"

"It took me a day to chop through that jungle, not twenty minutes," Levi defended. "I didn't even know about the tunnel until the following day. I was so mad at you for staying in the village I volunteered to use the machete in the point position most of the day. Then I spent the night having an anxiety attack."

"Sorry about that, man." Nicholas lowered his voice. "Seriously though, when you get married, you'll understand. You can't think about *anything* else besides her for days."

"I can barely think of anything else but her, and I've never even held her hand," Levi mumbled. "Nor am I going to. It's against their tradition for a man and woman to touch each other before marriage."

"Might wanna get in good with her daddy, then, because the way you two look at each other makes me think it ain't gonna be long before you *want* to touch each other."

"That sucks," Levi mumbled.

"Worth it," Nicholas said. "Speaking of..." Nicholas stood from his seat to welcome Becky with a quick kiss.

Becky sat with Nicholas but leaned across to smile at Levi. "Good morning."

"Good morning." Levi started shoving food to her side of the table, assuming she was just as hungry as her husband.

"Thank you, I'm starving." Becky opened the packet of tortillas. "Ooh, they're still warm."

"Yeah, the chief's wife is a fantastic cook, and she just keeps bringing out food." Levi had never felt so spoiled in his life. For all their talk about the scientists invading the village and threatening the temple pyramid, the villagers sure welcomed the group with open arms, or at least open kitchens. They still didn't seem to understand why the scientists were there in the first place, but hopefully they would in time.

"Please thank her for us," Becky said.

"She understands Spanish," Levi said. "You can tell her yourself. As soon as she realizes you're out here, she'll probably bring more food."

"Where is the chief?" Nicholas asked. "And Tiani."

"I don't know," Levi said. "I haven't seen them yet this morning."

"When do you want to go back over to the temple again?" Nicholas asked.

"I was just waiting for you." Levi shrugged.

"What if we didn't get out of bed again today?" Nicholas grinned.

"Then I would have been annoyed while I waited." Levi tried to keep a straight face but failed and chuckle-snorted.

"You two are seriously addicted to each other, aren't you?" Becky asked, her hand holding her fork in midair.

"Let me see if I can explain it," Nicholas said to his wife. "It's like ripping my heart out of my chest, throwing it over to the other side of the mound, and asking me to sleep over here and my heart to sleep over there. Am I wrong?" He turned to Levi.

"Not at all." Levi cringed. "Sorry, I just couldn't try to sleep over there again."

"You don't need to be sorry," Becky said. "I'm the idiot who married one half of an identical set of twins. I just didn't realize you were this extreme. How come *you* were able to sleep just fine?" She turned to Nicholas.

"You wore me out, woman." Nicholas leaned over for a kiss, and Levi fought the urge to gag.

"We just need to get your brother married off, and then we won't have this problem." Becky returned Nicholas's kiss.

"I'll get right on that," Levi grumbled, knowing the reality of his situation wasn't quite that easy. He either needed to ignore the connection he had with Tiani or find a way to live on two continents at the same time. "For now, we need to get to work. I'm sure the team is quite annoyed that their archaeologist, linguist, and science manager are all on the wrong side of the mound."

They finished eating, packed up some food and water to take with them to last through the day, grabbed some flashlights, and braved the scary, dark tunnel without the benefit of a guide. The scary, dark tunnel that allowed them to live in luxury while their team roughed it in the jungle. If sleeping in tents in the middle of a village that didn't have modern facilities, running water, or high-speed internet could be considered living in luxury.

Chapter Twenty-Nine

A Small Fortune

When Levi arrived at the temple pyramid with Nicholas and Becky, he learned the reason they couldn't find Tiani and Chief Gabor in the village was because the two tribal leaders were already at the temple site.

Levi felt an actual physical relief when he met Tiani's eyes for the first time that morning and noticed she seemed to sigh when seeing him too. The connection wasn't as strong as the one between him and his twin, but it was real nonetheless.

"About time," Timothy called out upon seeing them emerge from the tunnel. As excavation director for the archaeology team, he was standing with the tribal leaders around the makeshift conference table they had set up with equipment. From their frustrated expressions, Levi suspected they were struggling with the language barrier.

"Blame him, not me." Levi hitched his thumb toward his brother.

"Nah, blame my wife," Nicholas said. "She's the one who can't keep her hands off me."

"Hey," Becky said. Laughing, Becky pushed Nicholas so hard he fell into Levi. "I think you should blame the chief. He's the one who forced us to get married."

"Yeah, I can tell you're just devastated by the institution." Timothy rolled his eyes playfully.

Nicholas wrapped his arms around Becky and kissed the top of her head. "Marriage is absolute torture."

Levi noticed the confusion on Tiani and her father's faces and explained to them in Yucatec that their excavation director was teasing Nicholas and

Becky about being married. A little smile pulled at the corners of Tiani's lips, and then she pulled her face back into a mask of seriousness.

"Now that you are all here," Tiani said in Spanish to include everyone, "explain your invasion of our sacred temple." This wasn't a request. Tiani seemed to command attention and expected her subjects to fall in line to her demands. She was inherently regal before she knew she was royalty.

"Rebecca." Timothy turned to Becky. "Would you like to take the lead since you were the first to discover the Fibonacci spiral?"

They moved the conversation to the portable folding table where electronic equipment was spread out, fully charged by a small generator the drop team had delivered. Becky opened her laptop and displayed an aerial image of the Yucatan Peninsula zoomed in to the area around the temple pyramid.

Tiani picked up the computer, tipped it on its side, and looked behind it to see how it made that strange image. Finally, she sat back and folded her arms, her brow creased.

Without attempting a full explanation about spectral imaging and waves of light and how they were used to display the geographic region without vegetation, Becky showed two images of the same location, with trees and without trees.

Tiani and her father both gasped the same way Levi and Nicholas had the first time they'd seen the image. Even though they didn't understand the process, they understood enough to recognize their temple pyramid and their village at the center of the spiral of mounds.

"You know about this trading post over here by Tikal," Becky said, pointing to the screen. "And you know of this village over here on the other side of the jungle near El Zotz, but you might not know about all the other villages."

Becky zoomed out to show them Flores, then the entire Yucatan Peninsula, and Central America, then the continents of South and North America, then zoomed out so far that Google Earth showed the entire globe, which Becky could spin with the pointer of her mouse.

Levi could tell Tiani and Chief Gabor were overwhelmed. He backtracked, pulling the computer closer to him, and zoomed again into their village, then zoomed out just a little bit more to show them Tikal.

Speaking in their native Yucatec to help them understand, Levi said. "You have seen the village at Tikal, right? Have you seen how many of these beautiful carvings are still on their temple pyramid?"

"No." Tiani shook her head. "There are no carvings."

"Exactly," Levi said. "Bad people stole the carvings many years ago."

"Why would anyone want to steal them?" the chief asked, his gruff voice confused and angry.

"To sell them to museums and art collectors," Levi explained. "They are very special."

"That's why they need to stay on the temple." Tiani folded her arms across her chest definitively.

"We agree." Levi waved his finger between himself and the surrounding scientists. "We're here to document this building and translate the carvings so we can find a way to preserve the temple forever and stop looters."

"How?" she asked, narrowing her eyes.

"We don't know yet," Levi admitted. He looked up and spoke in Spanish again to include the others. "They want to know how we plan to preserve the temple and stop looters."

"We need to find some way to protect the land so that it's illegal to trespass," Nicholas answered, also in Spanish. "The government owns the land. I wonder if they would sell the whole area to the village. How much land is owned by the village?" Nicholas asked the tribal chief.

"People do not own land." Chief Gabor lifted his chin with pride. "Mother Earth owns the land."

"Well, the Guatemalan government *controls* this land," Levi said in a soft, soothing voice. "Once people learn about the temple, they will want to come and see the building for themselves. Unless we find a way to keep them off the land, people will try to force you to leave."

"We are the protectors of this temple," the chief said lifting his chest. "This has been the case for many generations. No one can force us to leave."

"It's happened in other parts of the world," Levi said. "Natives have been forced from their homes with much more powerful weapons than spears and swords. We don't want that to happen to you."

"We should purchase the land," Nicholas said matter-of-factly.

"That would cost a small fortune." Timothy shook his head dismissively.

"What else are we going to do with our money?" Nicholas asked. "Between our estate and the money from the Sayids, there has to be enough to convince the Guatemalan government."

"Not a bad idea." Levi caught his brother's vision. "We can purchase the land and deed it over to the tribe."

"Have you figured out yet how much money they have?" Timothy asked.

"No, we need to take them over to Flores and find that bank." Levi turned again to Tiani and the chief. "Do you have an easy way to get to Tikal? More tunnels, perhaps?"

"Yes, we have tunnels under every mound," Tiani said.

"Can you use the satellite phone to call for a Jeep?" Levi asked Timothy, his excitement growing.

"Forgive me for playing devil's advocate here," Kaden, the site administrator interrupted. "But aren't we here in Guatemala to conduct an archaeology expedition? Shouldn't we be examining the excavation site rather than taking a road trip to some bank an hour away?"

"If we don't preserve this land," Nicholas said. "There won't be a site for long. We may be the first team of scientists to venture this far into the jungle to study this pyramid, but we won't be the last. If we can document our findings to present to the scientific community, and preserve the land surrounding the site, we will hopefully prevent looters from destroying the sanctity of the building."

"NCALM may have been the first team of scientists to fly this region using LiDAR, but we won't be the last, especially after word gets out," Timothy said. "I agree with the twins on this one. If they're willing to fund the purchase of this land, we can't turn our backs on the notion."

Chapter Thirty

Miscommunication

"How long will it take to walk to Tikal?" Timothy asked Tiani and Chief Gabor, holding the satellite phone and maintaining his communication in Spanish. The temple pyramid behind him shined in the late-morning sun streaming through the tree canopy, reminding Levi why this trek to Tikal and then south to Flores was so important.

Chief Gabor glanced at his daughter, and they both shrugged. The chief answered in Spanish. "Four hours, maybe."

"Wow, a little different than a three-day trek over the mounds," Becky said. She seemed so relaxed since marrying Nicholas. She had literally let her hair down, almost to the point of looking disheveled. Levi knew his twin liked his wife this way. From the moment they'd met, she'd been poised and professional. But Nicholas had asked her to wear her hair down for their wedding, and she hadn't twisted it back up in its professional style since that day. She finally looked like the crazy scientist she was rather than a businesswoman.

"Maybe we should wait until tomorrow," Timothy suggested, hesitating with the satellite phone ready to call for the Jeeps. They planned to meet them at the edge of the jungle where the tribe exited near the trading post at Tikal.

"Yeah, we need that will and testament that Prince Marcos Sayid left for the chief's grandfather," Nicholas said. The paperwork was on the other side of the mound, separating the village from the temple pyramid. This pushed back the time of departure even further.

"And before traveling over there, we should research this bank a little more," Levi said. Knowing the will and testament had been written three generations prior gave him pause. "We need to make sure the bank actually exists before we drag the tribal leaders and a third of our excavation team away from the pyramid."

"Let's leave at first light tomorrow," Timothy suggested. "I'll have the Jeeps pick us up late morning in Tikal, and we'll try to return to the village before dark. This may be a long process to purchase the land surrounding the temple pyramid, possibly even several months, but at least we'll find out how much money we have to work with."

"That will give us the rest of today to prepare everything," Nicholas said, nodding in agreement.

Kaden, the site administrator interrupted. "What would you have the rest of us doing while the most important people on our team are missing? We're already days behind and running out of time before the rainy season starts."

"Our geoarchaeologist, Isaiah, can handle preparing each stela for capturing high-resolution photographs as well as, or better than, I can." Nicholas smiled fondly at Isaiah. "Every one of you should be using every digital device available to take the photographs, even your cell phones. They're not much good for anything else this far out in the middle of nowhere. Besides, you'd be surprised what detail shows up on one camera compared to another, plus differences in lighting, glare, shadows, shutter speed."

Levi added his thoughts. "Jeremiah, our finds manager can collect the data and organize the digital images the same way he would catalog bones and pottery fragments. All of you should be helping with soft brushes to clean the stela and prepare them for photographs. One of you use the drone to capture video and photographs of the upper most parts of the temple pyramid."

Nicholas jumped back into the instructions. "Every bit of data you collect will help us conduct analysis later. As an environmental archaeologist, and linguist, my and Levi's job will require a great deal of research to piece together the past and the present. The in-situ data collection is only the beginning."

"Okay, people." Timothy clapped his hands together once. "You heard the boss. Hop to it."

"Timothy, I thought you were the boss," Levi joked out of the side of his mouth.

Timothy patted Levi on the back and grinned. "He who has a billion dollars and offers to purchase a pyramid and the thousands of acres surrounding it... is the boss."

They all laughed, except the tribal leaders.

Levi turned to them and spoke in Yucatec. "We were just telling everyone on the team what to do while we're traveling to Flores to purchase your land."

"These people speak too many languages at the same time," Tiani said in Yucatec, folding her arms across her chest. The colorful handwoven textile dress she wore was designed to showcase her high standing in the tribe by accenting the feathers in her headdress of ornately carved wood. Her hair was pulled back and intricately braided around her headdress, then cascaded down her back. As he'd just been thinking of Becky letting down her hair, Levi wondered if Tiani would ever be willing to do the same. She nodded toward the team of scientists gathered around the computer table and glared at Levi. "They mix Spanish together with your English language, and we cannot understand them."

Levi realized most of the recent conversation had morphed into a passionate mix of English and some Spanish, and the tribal leaders were probably beyond lost. He spoke directly to them in Yucatec, hoping to bring them up to speed.

"We were telling the rest of the team to collect photographs of the whole temple so we can translate them, while we travel to Flores to purchase the land. This team of scientists who discovered your temple pyramid may have been the first, but they won't be the last. More scientists will come here if we don't find a way to make their presence illegal."

"Most of what you just said made no sense to me, even in Yucatec." Tiani pursed her lips and lifted her chin, her voice growing more animated. She stepped closer to Levi and pushed her hands against his chest. "I am tired of you giving me one sentence answers to translate an entire conversation. You need to translate better."

Levi was startled by her touch. His eyes fixed on hers, and his words, spoken slowly and in her native language, conveyed a meaning beyond science. "I will do whatever you ask of me, my princess."

She gave him one more shove, then seemed to realize what she'd done in touching Levi, and her eyes grew wide. She took a step back and stared at her traitorous hands. She tucked them behind her back, glanced at her father, and back at Levi.

"What the heck was that all about?" Nicholas asked in English, a near whisper, speaking only to his twin. "What did you just say to each other?"

"Uh… I'm not entirely sure." Levi still couldn't pull his gaze from Tiani's, and her perfect facade was completely broken. A tear ran down each of her cheeks, and she was shaking. "I think I may have just pledged myself to be her humble servant for the rest of eternity."

"Now you understand," Nicholas whispered, even closer to Levi and softer.

"Not quite the same," Levi whispered back. "The chief had a spear to your chest, insisting you marry Rebecca. He's going to have a spear to my back, running me out of his village."

"I don't think so," Nicholas mumbled. "Look at his eyes. He *respects* you."

"I can't."

"Can't what?"

"I can't pull my gaze away from hers," Levi said. "I'm making a fool of myself right now, aren't I?"

"Nah." Nicholas patted him on the back. "Anyone who doesn't understand has never been in love."

"Is that what this is?" Levi asked, his eyes glassy.

"You tell me," his twin challenged.

"I have no idea," Levi mumbled.

"Let's go purchase some land so you can prove yourself worthy of a Mayan princess," Nicholas said.

"Worthy…" There was no such thing. No man could ever be worthy of this woman.

Tiani interrupted the twins' whispered conversation, demanding in Yucatec, "You need to teach me English." Then she turned on her heel and stormed away.

Chapter Thirty-One

Your Quest Begins Now

"Why are you still standing here?" Nicholas hissed at Levi. "Go after her!"

Levi shook himself out of his trance, glanced at Tiani's father, whose face had a similar startled expression, then hurried to catch up to Tiani. She was heading toward the tunnel and entered the darkness before he could reach her.

"Tiani, wait," Levi called out in Yucatec. Neither of them had a lantern or flashlight, so they were plunged into near blackness almost immediately, and Levi plowed into her when she stopped. He grabbed her arms to hold her upright and keep himself from face-planting into the tunnel. He quickly pulled his hands off her arms. "I'm sorry!"

She spun around to face him and was suddenly close enough that he could have kissed her if he'd been so bold. He would never disrespect her that way.

As if the move was involuntary, Tiani lifted both hands and placed them on his chest again, leaving them there. Her breath had increased, and she glanced up into his eyes.

"Tiani," Levi whispered, not sure what else to say.

"My father will force me to marry you because I touched you."

"I would marry you this minute." Levi's hands moved as if on their own volition, and he rested them on her hips, his eyes searching hers. "But is that what *you* want? In my culture women have a choice who to marry."

"I do not live in your culture." She shook her head, not answering his question.

"I will speak to your father," Levi said, still with his hands on her hips and her hands on his chest. "As long as he knows that I'm *willing* to marry you, he won't force us. I'll tell him that I need time to prove to him that I'm worthy of his daughter. And then, once we get to know each other, if *you* want to marry me, I will marry you. But only if that's what *you* want. If you don't want to marry me, I will find a way to get you out of the commitment."

"How will I know if I want to marry you?"

"You'll feel a powerful pull toward me in your heart," Levi explained, realizing his hands had subtly pulled her closer. "You'll feel as if you want to be near me all the time." He was mostly describing how he felt about her.

"I feel that way already," she said. He suspected that.

"Let's continue to get to know one another and learn to communicate better, just without touching each other." Neither of them moved their hands.

"Will you still teach me English?" Her vulnerability was endearing.

"Of course," Levi whispered. "I will do anything for you, princess."

"Will you kiss me? Like a girlfriend?"

"After you marry me," he said, raising his eyebrows seductively. "I will not compromise you in any way."

"You are already touching me. That, according to our traditions, is compromising me." Her hands subtly kneaded his chest, reminding him that she had touched him first and still had her hands on him.

"I can't seem to pull my hands away." His words were barely a breath.

Her hands traveled up his shoulders to his neck and gently pulled him closer. Tempting. So tempting.

"Tiani, we mustn't do this." His willpower finally caught up to his brain, and he reached up to pull her hands from around his neck, holding them in his and lifting them to kiss her knuckles. She nearly fell into his arms. He caught her by the elbows and held her upright. "I don't want to cause you any more trouble. Let's go back out into the sun, and I'll talk to your father, okay?"

"Okay," she agreed with a sigh.

Before letting her go, Levi allowed himself one more tiny indulgence. He pulled her into his arms and she laid her head on his chest while he held her, breathing deeply to capture the scent of whatever natural oils she used to create the thickness and sheen of her chestnut hair. Around her crown, she wore a complex arrangement of braiding that cascaded down her back. She was elegant and regal and completely off-limits until the day they shared vows before the tribe, and the chief pronounced them married.

She took a step back and folded her arms across her chest as if forcing herself not to touch him again.

Levi tucked his hands behind his back like an old-fashioned gentleman and followed her out of the tunnel.

Without allowing his gaze to pull to the left or right, Levi strode directly toward Chief Gabor Sayid.

"Your highness, may I have a word with you?" Levi purposely looked him in the eye, lifting his chin and pulling bravery from somewhere deep inside.

The chief grunted and fell in line beside Levi, waiting to speak until they walked away from earshot of the others, not that any of them would understand Yucatec.

"Tiani has explained to me your tribe's requirement that she marry me after having placed her hands on my chest in such a familial way." Levi brought his own hand up to his chest as if demonstrating. "I am willing to take on the responsibility, but not until I prove myself worthy of your daughter. What would you have me do to prove my worth?" Levi waited, fearful the chief would force the marriage now, taking away Tiani's agency. Or worse, forbid Levi from seeing her again.

"I don't know," Chief Gabor said, turning to face him and looking him up and down. "You are not a warrior. How will you protect her?"

Levi wanted to list all the reasons she wouldn't need protection living in his world, but that would imply he intended to take Tiani from her home and force her to live his lifestyle.

What the heck was he doing? She would never leave her tribe, especially not for a geeky professor. What could she possibly see in him? Why was he pursuing a relationship with her when they could never make it work?

He would *find* a way to make this work. Somehow.

"I will use the skills of my intelligence to protect her." Levi pointed to his own head. "I may not be large in stature, but I am very smart. Search your heart and decide how you would like me to prove my worth. When you have come to a conclusion, tell me what you would have me do, and I will do that."

Levi bowed his head reverently to Chief Gabor, a prince in the Sayid royal bloodline, the man who would someday become his father-in-law. Lifting his gaze, Levi met the chief's eyes again and waited.

"I will search my heart and give you my decision at a later time," Chief Gabor said. "Your quest to prove your worth begins now."

The chief shouldered past Levi and strode with intention toward his daughter, who still waited by the entrance to the tunnel.

Before she followed her father back to the village, Tiani met Levi's gaze, and he nodded subtly, telling her in a nonverbal way that the chief had agreed to their plan.

She allowed a tiny smile to break her facade before pulling her features back into place and turned to follow her father.

Chapter Thirty-Two

Inevitable

L evi shuffled his way back to his team of scientists, wondering how they would react to the outdated tribal rules he'd just agreed to follow. All twelve of them waited with gaping mouths and wide eyes.

"First of all, what did you say that got Tiani so upset that she stormed away?" Nicholas asked. "And what happened in the tunnel? And what did you just say to her father?"

"Um... I am now officially on a quest to prove my worth to the tribal chief so that I'll be ready on my wedding day to protect his daughter forevermore," Levi answered his twin brother.

"You're engaged?" Becky stepped forward, an excited gleam in her eye. Having recently married Nicholas, she was still riding the high of true love. "That's so sweet."

"You'd think... but it's not that sweet when you consider the complete disregard for Tiani's choices in forcing her to marry me."

"Why would she be forced to marry you?" Nicholas asked.

"Because she touched me." Levi realized he'd need to explain things in better detail but was interrupted.

"Whoa, you move fast. How much fun did you have in that tunnel?" Matt asked. As the youngest member of their archeological team of scientists, he was also the least educated, still working his way through graduate school. "I thought you were just talking."

"We *were* just talking." Sort of. "She placed her hands on my chest when she got mad at us about speaking too many languages at the same time."

"That's what she got upset about?" Timothy asked. "That we were speaking too many languages?" Timothy led the team as excavation director, and was supposedly in charge, although Levi felt like the one in charge since he was the only one who could translate for the tribal members.

"She'd be forced to marry you because she put her hand on your chest?" Becky asked.

"Weren't we speaking enough Spanish?" Kaden asked. As site administrator, Kaden had fewer responsibilities than his title implied, although he interjected his opinions frequently, often saying what everyone needed to hear.

"Let Levi explain," Nicholas said, nodding for Levi to continue.

"In Houston you guys probably speak Tex-Mex all the time without even thinking about it," Levi said. "But here they only speak Spanish when trading at the outposts. That's not their primary language, and they can't keep up when you throw English words in with the Spanish."

"Yeah, we do speak Tex-Mex in Houston," Timothy admitted.

Levi continued his explanation. "Plus, everyone's talking to each other as if we're all a bunch of PhDs, which most of us are. So even the Spanish is over their heads."

"I hadn't thought of that," Nicholas said.

"Then after we talked and laughed for five minutes, I turned to her and translated that whole conversation with one dismissive sentence. That's when she lost her temper."

"Feisty little thing, ain't she?" Matt raised his eyebrows playfully. "I like that in a girl."

"That's my future wife you're talking about." Levi didn't crack a smile, although he mostly meant his statement to be lighthearted.

Matt's countenance shifted. "Sorry, man. I didn't mean anything by it."

"Are you really being forced to marry her?" Nicholas asked, true concern in the crease of his brow.

"No, she is being forced to marry me. There's a difference. But I'm delaying the inevitable by claiming I need to prove myself worthy. Tiani and I hope this will slow things down. We barely know each other. Plus, if she marries me, I want that to be *her* choice, not her father's choice, or because of some tradition. I want her to marry me because she wants to marry me."

"What about you?" Becky asked. "What if you don't want to marry her?"

Multiple guys in the group laughed at Becky. Nicholas pursed his lips together, obviously trying to hide a smile. Levi stuck his hands in his pockets and shuffled his feet.

"Don't you dare make some comment about her beauty or the fact that she's a princess or the daughter of a tribal chief." Becky put her hands on her hips.

"Relax, babe." Nicholas wrapped his arms around his wife. "I think we were all laughing in recognition of the fact that Levi has his tongue out like a faithful Labrador whenever she so much as glances his way."

"Yeah, Levi wanting to marry Tiani is about as obvious as Nicholas wanting to marry you," Timothy said. "He's whipped."

"Anyway..." Levi felt his cheeks heat as they laughed at him again. "Don't we have work to do? A temple pyramid to document?" He pushed past the team members and headed toward the majestic building, a tiny grin pulling at the corner of his mouth.

Chapter Thirty-Three

Take Me to Your Village

At first light, the small group was assembled and ready to hike to Tikal. Chief Gabor and Tiani had enlisted two of their warriors to accompany them, and Timothy had asked the expedition's field guide, James, to come along. Becky of course joined Nicholas, so that made nine people, including Levi. They would need two Jeeps to get from Tikal to Flores.

Trekking along ready-made trails and under the mounds using tunnels made the four-hour walk to Tikal seem easy compared to hacking through the jungle with a machete.

After the tension from the previous day, everyone kept their speaking brief and simple, and always in Spanish.

The previous evening at the campfire in the middle of the village, Levi and Tiani had developed a system of communicating where she would lift her eyebrows a certain way to tell him she had no idea what one of them was talking about and he would know to give her a better explanation in Yucatec.

They had also begun some very basic lessons of English, using things they could see in the circle of light from the campfire such as the words for tree, rock, foot, or hand. That morphed into simple phrases of salutations and declarations. My name is Tiani. I am hungry. I don't speak English.

She was an eager learner and picked things up quickly. Levi had no doubt Tiani would eventually be able to pick up the language.

Inevitably, the topic of their pseudo-betrothal came up, and Tiani thanked Levi for working with her father to deescalate the situation. He hoped to convey to her that he *did* want to marry her. He just wanted their marriage to be a choice rather than forced. Levi hoped she understood.

When they reached Tikal, they hurried into the waiting Jeeps, not wanting their unlikely group to be scrutinized by outside observers.

"Is this your first time in a car?" Becky asked Tiani since they sat together in the middle seat. Levi's ears perked up to hear the answer.

Tiani gripped the arm rest, her eyes wide and her body tense. "I don't know what this means."

Becky patted the seat beneath her and said, "This car will take us to the next village very quickly. We would not be able to walk so far in a day."

"Okay," Tiani said but didn't loosen her grip the entire hour drive from Tikal to Flores.

Levi fought the urge to hold out his hand and help Tiani down from the car just as Nicholas helped his wife Becky. He had promised not to touch Tiani again, but he wanted to be able to hold her hand, or touch her lower back, or give her a hug. Even that tiny level of intimacy would have to wait.

While Levi and Nicholas escorted Tiani and her father into the bank, Timothy took the rest of the group to a local shopping mall and to the island for sightseeing.

Walking into the bank was possibly the first time Tiani and Chief Gabor had experienced air conditioning, carpet, and electricity. The two confident tribal leaders drew closer together and Gabor protectively wrapped his arms around his daughter. Levi wished he could be the person to warm and comfort Tiani but relished in the tender moment between father and daughter. Then he stepped up to the accounts manager to request help from the bank.

Thankfully, one employee at the bank had a primitive understanding of Yucatec and the Mayan traditions. With Levi's ability to translate between three languages, and the twins' knowledge of the Sayid royal family, they were able to find the correct account from two generations prior. By some miracle, they were able to access the account even though Tiani and Chief Gabor had no formal identification.

The tribe had no need for cash, so they left all the money—just over two million U.S. dollars—in the bank account. Wishing to remedy the lack of identification, they headed next to the Superintendent of Tax Administration office.

Again, Levi's ability to translate between three languages was invaluable. There would be several hoops to jump through in order to obtain birth certificates, personal identification, and passports. The process might include a trip to Guatemala City to the office of the National Registry of Persons. Levi suspected he may need to call in some favors and bring down a private jet to fly from Flores to Guatemala City rather than make the nine-hour drive.

Levi wondered when his archaeological expedition had morphed into a civil liberties procurement expedition. He glanced over at the elegant Mayan princess, Tiani Sayid, daughter of His Highness, Mayan Chief Gabor Sayid, and knew his expedition changed the minute she yelled at him for understanding her language.

As if sensing his gaze, Tiani turned her face briefly in his direction, and he caught a tiny pull of her mouth that was almost a smile. He couldn't help the grin that spread across his face and his twin nudged him with an elbow.

They had arranged to have an afternoon meal at La Villa Del Chef on the west side of the island and stood on the outdoor patio, watching boats on the lake and waiting for the rest of the group to join them. Levi wasn't sure if the flutter in his stomach was because they'd skipped lunch or because Tiani had glanced his way.

"She's always so poised, isn't she?" Nicholas whispered. "Like she can't let her guard down for a second."

"You and Becky should join us at the campfire tonight after the rest of the village retires. She's like a different person." Levi sighed, and his shoulders relaxed, thinking of their long talks. "She laughs."

"No way!" Nicholas turned to Levi with incredulity in his countenance. "I cannot picture this scenario. I have every intention of joining you at the campfire this evening. May need to take a quick nap first so that I can stay awake."

"Yeah, right. I know what your version of a nap entails." Levi shuddered, not wanting to think about what his brother and Becky were doing so frequently.

"The way your little princess looks at you with those bedroom eyes, I have a sneaking suspicion you'll know first-hand sooner than later."

"What would Mother and Father say if we both come home married?"

"They will be excited to meet their new daughters-in-law," Nicholas answered.

"What about when they find out one of their daughters-in-law lives in Houston, and the other..." Levi hesitated. Was this really happening?

"Moving down here, aren't you?" Nicholas whispered.

"I don't see any other way of making this work," Levi said.

"We're wealthy enough that you can have a home in Houston and one in Guatemala," Nicholas said. "Like snowbirds who live in Michigan half the year and Florida half the year."

"We're not talking about driving across the country here," Levi said. "This is a different continent."

"So, let's purchase a private jet," Nicholas suggested. "We can all travel back and forth any time we want. Come down for research expeditions, come home to the States because we've been detached from each other's hips for too many hours. Bring our parents down for a weekend getaway." Nicholas pointed down the beach to the fancy hotel next door.

"You really think it's doable?" Levi gulped, feeling vulnerable.

Nicholas pulled his shoulder around so Levi would look at him. "We can do anything we put our minds to. We're the geek twins."

"Even purchase thousands of acres of land surrounding a pyramid in the middle of a jungle?" Levi asked with a grin and a tiny bit more hope.

"Yeah, like that." Nicholas looked over Levi's shoulder, then smiled and pushed past him to run ahead and grab his wife in a hug.

"Seriously?" Levi muttered to himself. "They've been apart for two hours. You'd think they hadn't seen each other in months."

"Translate for me?" Tiani came up beside him, and they stood side by side, watching Nicholas swing Becky in a hug. He knew she wasn't asking him to translate what Nicholas was saying to the rest of the group who had finally joined them at the restaurant. She wanted to know what Levi and his brother had been saying to each other in English.

"Nicholas thinks I should move to Guatemala," Levi whispered in Yucatec. They were far enough away from her father, who was leaning against the railing watching the boats, for him to hear.

"What if I want to move to America?" Tiani asked. They were still standing together and apart from the others, and her pinky finger brushed his, purposely. Levi glanced toward her father, noting he was still facing the other direction.

"We don't have to choose," Levi said. "We can have two homes. One here in your village..." He hesitated and finally turned to her, searching her eyes.

"And one in yours?" she whispered.

"Yeah." His nod was subtle. "One in mine."

"Does your village have a lot of trees?" Tiani asked.

"Not as many as yours. But I could take you all over the world and show you places with many trees and places with no trees, and places where other people speak Yucatec, and places where neither of us will understand the languages."

"But you speak *three* languages." She creased her brow. "Are there more?"

"Many, many more."

"Levi?" She lowered her gaze and bit her lip.

"Yes?" He gulped.

"I feel the way you tell me I should feel," she said. "I feel pulled to you, and I want to be with you. You said that is all I need to feel in order to know I want to marry you."

Levi wanted to tell her there were so many more things she needed to know, but he didn't want to dissuade her. She would have a great deal more to learn about his world, but she would have to experience his world in order to understand. "Tiani, do you want to marry me?"

"Yes." She nodded but kept her face lowered.

Glancing over to her father again to ensure the chief was still facing away, Levi boldly raised his hand and lifted her chin with his finger. How badly he wanted to lean down and press his lips to hers, but he didn't dare. He was already crossing a line by touching her chin. "I want to marry you too."

She visibly relaxed, and Levi's heart raced in excitement and anticipation. She wanted to marry him. He couldn't believe his own luck.

"I'll speak to your father," Levi said. "I'll ask him if I've proven myself worthy of you."

"If you take me to your village, am I allowed to decide that for myself?"

He chuckled. "Yes, you would be allowed to decide."

"Then I want to go there. I want to tell *your* father that you are worthy."

"I want you to meet my family." Levi nodded. "Maybe I can bring them here for our wedding. But, either way, I think your father will decide I am worthy. Especially if you tell him you think I am. Your words mean a great deal to him."

"Will you still take me to your village?"

"Yes, princess, I will take you to my village."

Levi noticed the group coming in their direction, ready to head into the restaurant, and he stepped away from Tiani. He purposely sat at the opposite side of the table, right next to her father, where he knew he wouldn't be tempted to hold her hand... or do anything else.

Chapter Thirty-Four

Separate Lives

After they had a jovial lunch regaling what the others had missed while they were separated, their next stop was the Registry of Catastral Information to obtain maps and surveys of the land surrounding the temple pyramid. In order to purchase the land, they needed as much information as possible about the specific ownership of the land, the extent, value and tax valuation. They knew the purchase would take months, if not years, to finalize, but at least they had a starting place.

A thought kept tickling the back of Levi's mind that being married to the daughter of the tribal chief could provide an advantage when attempting to purchase the land. He knew foreigners were allowed to purchase land in Guatemala, but this was a huge chunk of land that was currently owned by the federal government and occupied by natives who were basically living there for free. The opportunity to receive tax revenue from the owner of the land may be another incentive.

Other thoughts plagued him as they drove north from Flores to Tikal. An hour in the back-row seat of a large Jeep, staring out the window as the landscape rolled by, gave him time to think.

Tiani and Becky again sat together in the middle row, and Levi sat beside Nicholas. The chief sat in the front passenger seat beside the driver. None of them held any conversations until Nicholas leaned closer and spoke in a voice just loud enough to be heard by Levi.

"You doing okay?" His twin was perceptive.

"A lot on my mind, that's all." Levi picked at his fingernails, his hands resting in his lap.

"Anything you want to talk about?" Nicholas asked.

"Just trying to figure out how I'm going to make this all work."

"What were you and Tiani talking about while I was trying to distract everyone else before lunch?"

"Kind of making our engagement a little more official," Levi said. "I'm planning to talk to her father either tonight or tomorrow and see if he has decided if I'm worthy to marry his daughter."

"After all you did for them today, I don't see how he could argue," Nicholas said.

"That's not why I helped them." Levi didn't mean to sound defensive.

"I know that, but the chief will probably see that to your advantage."

"I want to bring Mom and Dad down here for our wedding," Levi said. "I don't want ours to be the way yours was. I want the ceremony to be planned and spiritual and solemn, a celebration of our love and our *choice* to get married. You know what I mean?"

"You know what's funny," Nicholas said. "When Becky and I were standing there with the chief dictating the words that were said and the conch shells and the incense burning, I thought to myself that *you* would love this."

Levi chuckled. "As much as we think we're so identical, there are some ways in which we are very different."

"The minute we popped out of Mom, we immediately began separate lives, separate experiences," Nicholas said.

"I'm really gonna miss you when we're apart." Levi's throat tightened, and tears pricked his eyes.

"We'll never be more than an airplane ride away from each other, and you can have a satellite phone and call me every day if you want."

"I'll try not to bug you *every* day," Levi said.

"No way, man. You'd better call me every day, or I'll feel withdrawals. That or get super worried that you're alive and well."

"If you insist." Levi felt a weight lift from his shoulders knowing his twin *wanted* to hear from him every day. He didn't feel so alone. They still had over a month together before going back to the States. Separation anxiety this far in advance was not a good sign.

The four-hour trek from Tikal to the village was grueling after their long, tiring day. There was very little talking or excitement or anticipation, other than the desire to collapse into bed when they arrived. That got Levi thinking of another aspect of marrying Tiani. Where would they sleep?

He wondered if Tiani had her own home or if she expected they would live with her parents. That didn't seem like a fun place to spend their honeymoon. He wished he could take her back to their townhouse in Cambridge. Now that Nicholas was married, he'd likely move to Houston immediately to move in with Becky. Levi and Tiani would have the townhouse to themselves. The thought made him smile. That led his mind down other paths of anticipation, and he tried not to let his fantasies run too far amiss.

Tiani was not only elegant and beautiful, but there was a subtle fire behind her eyes that she saved only for him. Nicholas had described her as having bedroom eyes. Levi wondered if that was true. He wondered if maybe Tiani was fantasizing about him the same way he was fantasizing about her. He wished he could ask her. He wasn't even sure how to broach the subject.

Excuse me, Tiani, I know you said you'd like to get married. Have you thought about our wedding night at all? Do you have any idea how incredible that will be? Do you even know what men and women do on their wedding night? What kind of sex education did you have in school? School? That's where you go to a building to have teachers who instruct you how to read and write and do math. No school in the village? Ugh... okay. Guess you haven't had that particular health education class, huh? Gee, I'd be happy to teach you everything you need to know. No, I haven't been married before, but I have a general idea of how things work. We'll learn together.

Levi couldn't hide his grin and was glad they were walking single file along the jungle path. Explaining his train of thought, even to his twin, would be extremely embarrassing. He also entertained himself, thinking of all the other things he could teach Tiani, like how to speak English, how to interpret the symbols on the temple pyramid, how to read and write. Maybe he could even teach the other tribal members the same things. Maybe he was brought to this place at this time to help these people.

By the time they reached the village, his brain was tired along with his body. He mumbled goodnight to everyone else in their little group before collapsing in his tent. He didn't wake up until mid-morning, and he awoke to a surprise.

Levi nearly jumped out of his skin when his eyes opened and he found Tiani sitting cross-legged and serene near his feet, inside his tent, beside his bedroll. He glanced at the zipper door of the tent and wondered how she possibly got all the way in the door and zipped it closed without him waking.

"What are you doing in here?" Levi scrambled to a sitting position, tangled in blankets. "Your father is going to *kill* me."

"He already left with Timothy and James through the tunnel to the temple."

"Did anyone else see you come in here?" His racing heart hadn't yet slowed.

"I don't think so," she said.

"What are you doing in here?" Levi circled back to his original question.

"I spoke with my mother and father this morning," she said, not really answering his question. "I told them that you are worthy to be my husband, and they agree."

"They do?" Levi forgot his convictions and took her hands in his, excitement filling his heart.

"You were right that my father respects my opinion, but he also agreed with me before he heard my opinion. He sees something special in you, just like I do. He also knows that I will leave with you, but he knows I will return soon."

Levi was dumbfounded and didn't know how to answer. He fought every urge inside him not to pull her into his arms and kiss her until neither of them could see straight. Instead he answered her with a jumbled train of thoughts. "I want to bring my parents down for our wedding, and I want to take you home to Cambridge when the rainy season starts, and do you have a house here in the village for us to live? Or would you like to move into my tent? How soon can we get married? As soon as my parents can get here? Tomorrow, maybe? How many children do you want to have? Can I kiss you now?"

Tiani giggled. "That was a lot of questions. Yes, I have a house to sleep in with you. Yes, we can get married as soon as your parents arrive, even if that is tomorrow. As many babies as our bodies create together. And, no, you cannot kiss me until you marry me."

"Oh, how I wish I could marry you right now." Levi's inappropriate thoughts about his incredible fiancée were halted in another realization. "We need to hurry and go to the temple site so I can use Timothy's satellite phone and call my parents. The sooner they get here, the sooner I can kiss you."

"You go eat breakfast," Tiani said, grabbing his blanket and pulling it close to her chest. "I will lay here and wrap myself in your scent." She laid her head on his pillow, and he nearly lost his resolve.

Levi reached for the tent zipper and hurried out of his tent before he did something crazy like lie next to her and kiss her while slowly removing that dress. Breakfast. Not exactly what he was hungry for, but that would have to do for now. He zipped the tent closed behind himself and practically ran toward the breakfast hut.

Chapter Thirty-Five

Daughters-In-Law

"Hey, Mom, great to hear your voice," Levi said into the speaker of the satellite phone. "I have Nicholas with me. Is Dad home too? We want to talk to both of you."

"Oh! My boys! How are you? Yes, Dad is here. I'm hurrying to the other side of the house to find him. I think he's watching a baseball game in the den. Are you still in Guatemala?"

"Yep, we're still here," Levi said, glancing up at the colossal pyramid temple a few steps away from him, cleverly concealed by a jungle canopy so thick no explorer would find its location without the use of modern-day LiDAR technology.

"Hi, Mom," Nicholas said.

"Oh, Nick! How are you?"

"I'm good. We have some great news, but we want to tell you both at the same time."

"Henry! The boys are on the phone!"

Levi loved how his mom still called them "her boys" even though the twins were thirty years old.

"Put it on speakerphone so we can both hear," their dad said. "Hey, guys, how are you?"

"Good, Dad, how are you?" Levi asked.

"The Red Sox are winning," their dad said. "Can't get any better than that."

"How about a couple of daughters-in-law?" Nicholas asked. "Would that be better than the Red Sox winning?"

Their mom squealed so loud the noise caught the attention of some of the scientists on the other side of the clearing where they were documenting stelae.

"Emilie, calm down," their dad said. "We knew they'd eventually find women crazy enough to marry them. Did you guys find a set of identical twins?"

"Nope, Becky and Tiani couldn't be more different from each other," Nicholas said. "Polar opposites."

"Ooh, ooh! Let me guess," their mom said. "Becky is engaged to... Levi, and is a brunette with adorable freckles and works for, like, the Peace Corps or something that deals with humanitarian things."

Becky giggled and spoke up. "Hello, Mrs. Stephenson, this is Becky. I can't wait to meet you. Sadly, you are wrong on pretty much everything you just said."

"Oh! You sound so beautiful!" their mom said. "You can call me Emilie. Tell me everything about yourself!"

"Okay, well, my full name is Dr. Rebecca Benson. I have a PhD in Geography & Environment, I work at the University of Houston in the National Center for Airborne Laser Mapping, but I met Nicholas when we were both grad students at Boston University. I'm blonde with blue eyes, and we got married five days ago."

"Married?" she shrieked again. "You eloped and didn't tell me?"

"Calm down, Mom," Nicholas said. "There was a very good reason why we had to get married immediately."

"You got her pregnant?" their dad said with an air of disappointment. "Have I taught you nothing about protection?"

"Actually, we waited until we were married for that." Nicholas sounded annoyed. "Not that it's any of your business."

"Your son was a perfect gentleman, Captain Stephenson." Becky impressively remembered to include their father's high commission in the Army. "We were strongly encouraged to get married by the local Mayan tribal leader, and he performed the ceremony himself."

"Is that even legal?" their dad asked.

"Maybe..." Becky bit her lower lip and turned the conversation back over to Nicholas.

"Probably not," Nicholas said. "Which is why her parents are scheduling us a real wedding next month where Becky can wear a white dress, and have friends and family surrounding us, and pictures and flowers and cake."

"I do love cake." Becky giggled again.

"I love *you*," Nicholas whispered, and they leaned closer to give each other a quick peck.

Levi took that as his cue to change the subject. "Do you guys want to hear about Tiani now?" Levi heard the emotion in his own words, and he smiled at the elegant woman by his side. She had no idea what he just said, other than her own name.

"Yes, tell us about Tiani," their mom said. "I'm not even going to try to guess anything since apparently I'm so far off I'm on the wrong continent."

"Actually, you are on the wrong continent," Levi said. "Tiani was born in a small village in Guatemala and is the daughter of our previously mentioned Mayan tribal leader, His Highness, Prince Gabor Sayid."

There was no sound from his parents for a long moment, and Levi wondered if the line had gone dead. Finally, their dad cleared his throat. "Did you say... Sayid?"

"Yes, sir, I did," Levi said with respectful confidence. "My future father-in-law is the great-grandson of Prince Marcos Sayid of Madain Saleh, father to Prince Benjamin."

"No flippin way," their dad said. Levi was impressed how well his father hid the inappropriate word he would have used if he'd been talking with a group of soldiers instead of his wife and sons.

"So you're not married yet?" his mom asked. "Can you still get out of the engagement? I don't want you moving to some jungle village in a third world country. I've been there, and it's not pretty."

"Mother, Tiani is standing right next to me. Thankfully, she doesn't speak English, so she wouldn't have understood the insulting way you just dismissed her. I'm going to encourage her to say hello to you in Spanish, since you likely wouldn't understand her native Yucatec. I would encourage you to be polite, if not welcoming."

Levi turned to Tiani and invited her to say hello to his parents in Spanish.

"Hola me alegro de conocerte," Tiani said. "¿Hablas español?"

"Si, Nosotros hablamos español." Their father confirmed that they could understand her speaking Spanish. Then he told her they were glad to meet her as well.

"Anyway, you'll have a chance to meet her in person when you come down for our wedding," Levi said.

"Wait, what?" their mom stopped him. "You want us to come down *there* for you to get married?"

"Yes, ma'am," Levi choked out, no longer confident his parents would join him on what should be the happiest day of his life.

"When?" she squeaked out.

"Tomorrow, if possible." Levi met his twin brother's gaze, and Nicholas inherently knew it was his turn to interject.

"Mom, Dad, it's Nicholas," he said. "This is important to us. We'd really like for you to join us. But Levi's getting married tomorrow whether you're here or not." Nicholas nodded to Levi in confirmation. At least the most important member of Levi's family would be at his side.

Tiani brazenly tucked herself into Levi's arms, and he pulled her close, letting a tear or two fall into her beautiful hair. He wanted to reassure her that *she* wasn't the problem.

"They don't want me to move to Guatemala," Levi said in Yucatec, so only she understood him. "They will miss me."

"We can go visit them," Tiani said, looking up at him with innocence in her deep brown eyes.

"Yes, we can." Levi fought the overwhelming urge to lean down and kiss her. He was already crossing about a hundred lines by holding her in his arms and kissing the top of her head. One more day. He only had to wait one more day. And then he could kiss her every minute of every day from now until eternity.

"We can't just uproot our lives and fly off to Guatemala at a moment's notice, you know," his mom said.

"That's okay, Mom," Levi said. "We understand. Hey, I gotta go. I have... uh... work to do. I'll let you talk to Nick." He didn't even wait for his parents to say goodbye, just kept one arm around his bride's shoulders and walked with her toward the tunnel, intending to speak to her father and schedule their wedding for the following day.

Levi's happiness with Tiani wasn't contingent upon the approval of his parents. But he needed to obtain approval from *her* parents or there wouldn't be a wedding at all.

Chapter Thirty-Six

Last Minute Advice

As if drawn by a magnet, Levi spent the morning before his wedding walking the perimeter of the temple pyramid, gathering courage and peace for the day to come. He considered the stories that played out across the stelae. He already had a rough translation in mind for most of the carvings and could piece together the rest with context clues.

Once he had a bit of time—probably post-honeymoon—he planned to sit down with his four books of codices and really hash out the deeper meanings. Moving to Guatemala would actually give him the chance to absorb the energy of his surroundings as he translated. There was something to be said for looking at the stelae side by side rather than a picture at a time.

He still couldn't shake the notion that there was a Biblical connection. Nicholas always wanted to shove aside any references to the spiritual realm as the Mayan's worshiping the sun. But Levi had read too much of the text to dismiss a reference to God, if such a being existed.

Levi wasn't sure what he believed. He just knew that he'd evaluated religions all over the world through his study of linguistics and there were too many similarities between all of them to discount a connection. If the ancient Mayans were isolated pagans, as some people liked to believe, how did they know so much?

He ran his fingers along the ridges and valleys of the carvings as if he could find a deeper understanding by using a tactile method of reading, like braille to a blind person. He even closed his eyes as he walked.

Something made him stop on one particular stela, and he gazed at the carving with keener interest. He could see why some people assumed the

Mayans worshiped the sun. This carving almost looked like an exploding sun with rays of light radiating outward from the center.

Maybe not a sun. Maybe a star. An exploding star? Could happen. People saw meteor showers and comets all the time. Why not an exploding star?

Moving on, he found another stela that depicted people in agony, faces deformed with remorse or fear. Another stela showed a man in bondage, arms tied behind his back. Many of the stela showed great wars and sufferings. One stela seemed to represent prosperity with grains and fruits. Some stela showed earthquakes, storms, crumbled buildings, cities on fire.

He didn't want to look anymore.

Levi slumped to the ground and sat with his back against the wall of the temple pyramid, feeling a peace and happiness just from being in this place.

Just a few weeks ago he'd been working as a professor in a classroom filled with more people than those who lived in the whole village where he was about to take up permanent residence.

There were no cell phones here, no electricity, no microwave ovens. He had a solar charger and a generator, which he would keep using as a way of charging his electronic devices, his only means of data collection while here. He would have a satellite phone for emergencies and to contact his family.

Family. What did that even mean anymore? His own mother and father would not be attending his wedding. Maybe he should postpone the wedding until a later date so his parents could be here, or until he and Tiani could go there to the States.

Then his mind's eye conjured up her beautiful face and her sweet countenance when no one else was around to see her let down her stoic facade. The face she only allowed him to see. The face he had fallen in love with.

In a few short hours, that incredible woman would be his wife. No way was he postponing the chance to finally kiss her and touch her, not even in a sexual way, just to be able to hold her hand, wrap his arms around her, and yes, okay, he'd admit it, he wanted her in a very sexual way. A soft smile played across his lips, and he leaned his head back against the limestone to his back, closing his eyes and imagining what that would be like.

"There you are." A soft voice woke Levi from his daydreaming. Nicholas. The man who looked identical to him. The man who had stood by his side every day of his life since the moment they were conceived.

Conception. What a concept. Levi wondered if nine months from tonight he'd be holding his first child. He wasn't sure how fast these things worked, but he knew Tiani wouldn't be on the pill like Becky was. He had no other form of protection with him in the middle of the jungle, nor did he really want any. If a baby was meant to become part of his life, then he would welcome the addition.

"Were you napping?" Nicholas asked, lowering himself to the ground by Levi's side.

"Nah, just thinking, pondering how my life's about to change."

"Are you okay with this?" his brother asked. "You don't have to marry her if you don't want to. No one's forcing you."

Levi scoffed. "Heck yeah, I want to marry her. That feisty little minx captured my heart the first time she got in my face and yelled at me. She had me wrapped around her little finger on day one."

Nicholas chuckled. "Yes, she did."

"I was just thinking how I might be a father nine months from now," Levi said.

"How do you feel about that?" Nicholas asked.

"I think I'd like being a dad." Levi stopped when his throat caught. "Sure wish our dad was going to be here."

"We didn't exactly give them a heads-up in advance," Nicholas reminded them.

"I know." Levi nudged his twin's shoulder. "At least I told them in advance."

"That was not my fault." Nicholas held up his hands in surrender. They both chuckled and settled into a companionable silence. "Hey, have you thought about what you were going to wear tonight?"

"Well, I've got the clean clothes in my bag or the ones I'm wearing. I guess I'll change into my clean clothes. Probably should go take a bath first, huh?"

"Definitely." Nicholas stood and reached down to help Levi off the ground.

"Any last-minute advice for your completely inexperienced little brother?" Levi asked, brushing off his backside from where he'd sat on the jungle floor.

"Just have fun, man. Shoot, I was just as inexperienced as you," Nicholas said.

"At least you'd kissed Becky prior to marrying her," Levi said. "How do you approach intimacy with someone who has never had any formal education?"

"How do you know she's never had any education? Maybe her mom sat her down and gave her every detail she needs to know to prepare for her wedding night. Maybe she'll know more than you do. This is a completely different culture. They may not have high schools and universities, like we do, but they're smart. Very smart."

"True." Levi sighed. They started toward the tunnel. "I'm getting nervous over nothing, aren't I?"

"Not over nothing," Nicholas said. "These are the same fears every groom has the morning before his wedding. Of course, who am I to say? I didn't even know I was getting married the morning of my wedding." Nicholas chuckle snorted.

"You're such a geek." Levi laughed at his twin.

"Takes one to know one." Nicholas wrapped his arm around Levi's shoulders and pulled him in the direction of the tunnel. "Come on, let's get you ready for the best night of your life."

Chapter Thirty-Seven

Guests of Honor

What was taking so long? Levi fidgeted, standing at the center of the village, near where he and Tiani usually sat beside the community campfire each evening. An arbor of sorts had been decorated near the edge of the clearing, and incense burned lazy plumes of smoke all around.

He hadn't seen Tiani since the previous evening when some women, including her mother, had guided her away to prepare her for her wedding. Maybe Nicholas was right. Maybe Tiani would know more about what to expect than he did.

This wedding was a much bigger event than the hastily prepared and forced union between Becky and Nicholas. The tribe's princess was getting married. The daughter of the chief.

Oh my gosh! What the heck was he doing marrying the daughter of the chief? He didn't have the proper bloodline to be marrying a princess! He started sweating and grew nauseated. He took several deep breaths. He asked himself again, what was taking so long?

Most of the tribe and the team of scientists stood or sat nearby. Everyone else was waiting also, but they didn't seem nearly as nervous. Nor should they. He was the only man in this village who would be getting married today. If his bride ever showed up.

Maybe she would bail. Maybe she had already run off into the jungle, crying for this crazy, American geek to stop crushing on her. Maybe her mother and father were in their home right now discussing how best to break the news to him. How best to tell Levi that their daughter had changed her mind and didn't want to marry him.

Nicholas had long since stopped trying to calm him down, and Levi had long since stopped asking what was taking so long. He felt a sincere sense of remorse to his parents for all the times he'd ever muttered the annoying phrase, "Are we there yet?" while driving in a car.

Levi's attention was pulled in the complete opposite direction from where he expected to see Tiani appear when a conch shell sounded from somewhere far away in the jungle.

"Finally," Nicholas said, stepping to Levi's shoulder. "I thought they wouldn't get here in time."

Levi was confused. Why would there be some sort of wedding procession from down the jungle path? That wasn't even in the direction of the temple pyramid or anything sacred. More in the direction they would take if heading into one of the trading villages near Tikal. The conch shell sounded again, closer this time.

"They made it," Chief Gabor said in Spanish. Levi startled to find the chief at his other shoulder. Maybe he was worried his daughter had changed her mind as well.

When the procession drew closer to the edge of the clearing, Levi began to see men, warriors, at least five of them, no wait, there was one smaller person, a woman. Thank goodness. He couldn't wait to see his bride. Not sure why she would be trekking in from the jungle surrounded by warriors. This must be part of some ritual the tribe had.

"I'm so glad they came," Chief Gabor said in Yucatec, his words filled with emotion. "You deserve to have *your* family here at the time when you are joining yourself to *my* family."

"Huh?" Levi turned to his soon-to-be father-in-law. The chief offered a rare smile and put his hands upon Levi's shoulders, turning him back around to face the incoming procession.

The woman in the procession was not Tiani. Levi's breath caught. "Mom?"

Levi took off running in the direction of the group of warriors as soon as he realized the two people at the protected center were his parents.

"Dad? Mom? You made it!" Levi flung himself into their arms, tears pouring down his face. "You made it. You made it." His words caught in his throat as sobs racked through his body. His whole family was here.

His parents had left their home in Massachusetts, taken several connecting flights, driven at least an hour and trekked four hours on foot through a jungle to make it here in time for his wedding.

No wonder the wedding had been delayed. They were waiting for two very special guests of honor to arrive. Now that his parents were here, Levi was anxious to get this wedding started. But where was Tiani?

Chapter Thirty-Eight

Lost in Translation

After emotional greetings and introductions between the twins' parents and everyone on the science team, including Becky, their new daughter-in-law, everyone agreed to hold off any further excitement until their other daughter-in-law joined them.

Levi wiped tears from his cheeks as his twin brother led him to stand beneath the arbor that had been prepared for the wedding. As if everyone else had known they were waiting and had just been holding back, all of them took their places near the arbor. Chairs were moved closer and everyone just seemed to get settled. No more waiting.

More conch shells sounded, and all heads turned in the direction of the largest home in the village, that of Chief Gabor Sayid, who stood at Levi's side. Together they watched as his daughter, Princess Tiani Sayid, emerged through the front door.

A spotlight from heaven seemed to shine down on this elegant woman drawing closer with each step. Tiani's traditional Mayan gown was deep purple with bright pink and green trims, matching the feathers in her crown. Her hair had been braided even more intricately than usual, piled high and cascading down her back.

Her stoic, aloof expression faltered the briefest of seconds when she met his eyes, but like a trained royal, she pulled her mask back into place and kept her chin high. Her approach seemed to last forever, and yet flew past, and suddenly she was standing before him, gazing into his eyes. Nothing in the world had ever been more beautiful than this woman.

The only person capable of translating the words the chief spoke was the man who was tongue-tied at the altar, only half-listening to the magical words that would forever tie him together with his princess.

Levi didn't care if the Americans couldn't understand the vows spoken entirely in Yucatec. These words were for him and Tiani. Everyone else could listen with their hearts because he wasn't taking the spirit away from the ceremony by translating.

Chief Gabor called upon mother earth and the sky and the elements of nature, asking permission from the four cardinal points to join Levi and Tiani as husband and wife. He handed them each a seed.

"This represents the starting of your new life together," the chief said in Yucatec. "I bless you with abundance, love, and positive intentions. When you cast these seeds upon the land and into the water, you will obtain your wishes for your marriage."

They walked together around the arbor to a small cenote where Tiani cast in the seed in her hand. A small patch of soil had been prepared near the cenote where Levi cast his seed. The earth and water would accept their offerings.

The ceremony ended with women from the tribe tossing rose petals over Tiani and Levi as a way of dropping positive intentions. The women then danced around them to the beat of drums and blowing conch shells, and everything eventually morphed into a celebration where everyone was dancing and smiling and laughing.

There was never a moment where the chief pronounced them as man and wife nor did he invite Levi to kiss his bride. Levi wasn't sure if they were officially done with the ceremony as he was swept up in the festivities. But he smiled and laughed along as the tribal members lifted him and Tiani onto their shoulders and carried them around the village campfire and back around to the arbor, everyone dancing and chanting and clapping along.

Finally, they were placed on the ground again, together by the arbor, and Levi leaned closer to Tiani, asking if he was allowed to kiss her yet. In answer to his question, Tiani leapt into his arms and threw her arms around his neck and pressed her lips to his as if she'd been waiting her whole life for that moment.

As Levi deepened the kiss with his new bride, the thought occurred to him that this was his first kiss ever, and Tiani's first kiss ever, and they were sharing that moment together, sealing a lifelong commitment to never kiss any other person besides each other for as long as they both lived.

When they finally released their kiss, Levi pulled Tiani into his arms and held her, tears pouring down his face, their arms wrapped so tightly around each other he wasn't sure they'd ever let go.

The first person Levi saw when he finally released his bride was the man who was his mirror, his twin, his other half, his best friend. As Tiani's mother pulled her into an embrace, Nicholas pulled Levi into his arms, hugging him close, both smiling through tears.

Their mom pulled them apart and dragged Levi closer to Tiani so he could introduce them. They didn't understand most of what the other said, but they embraced as if they'd known one another all their lives and were long-lost friends, kindred souls. Their father was the next person to hug Tiani as their mothers hugged one another.

The dancing and celebrating and hugging and crying eventually shifted into an outdoor feast complete with roasting meats and flavorful vegetables and tortillas and corn breads and chocolate drinks. Levi didn't eat much. He didn't want to overindulge and be uncomfortable later. He wanted this night to be perfect.

Eventually Levi took the time to explain to his family the words that had been spoken during the ceremony and to talk about plans for the upcoming days and weeks. He told Tiani that he planned to say everything he needed to say in English so that he could tell them quickly and then spend the rest of the night with her. She liked that idea and chose that time to spend a few minutes with some of her close friends and family.

Nicholas promised that he and Becky, and the team of scientists, would entertain their parents the following day, taking them to see the temple pyramid and explaining the work they were doing there. Their mom and dad would sleep in a tent that night and the following night, then the next day the twins, their wives, and their parents would make the four-hour trek over to Tikal. They planned to show their parents around the ancient ruins at Tikal, then drive down to Flores and spend the night in a fancy hotel on the island.

Although the party was still in full swing, Levi said an official goodnight to his family, all of them understanding that he and Tiani would eventually just slip away and be gone for the night. They intended to have a nice dinner together the following evening.

Levi and Tiani spent the next several hours talking with guests and family, conversing whenever possible in Spanish when anyone nontribal was involved in the conversation. He and Tiani sat with Levi's parents for a long time getting to know them.

At one point, Levi's mom caught his attention and told him in English that Tiani was perfect, absolutely perfect.

When the crowd began to thin, something shifted between Levi and Tiani, an almost unspoken understanding that it was time for them to leave. Everyone else could fend for themselves. They wanted to be alone.

Chapter Thirty-Nine

A Sensitive Collection of Nerve Endings

Awkward. That's how Levi felt standing just inside the door of their tiny cottage near the outskirts of the village. They were actually quite close to where Nicholas and Becky still had their tent set up but had no intention of seeing them anytime soon.

Tiani excitedly showed Levi around the cottage, where she had already moved her belongings and his, tucking things away into cupboard spaces in the walls. There wasn't really a kitchen because the villagers ate in a communal fashion near the large eating area. But some corn breads and flatbreads and tortillas had been placed upon a shelf with fruits and nuts and jugs of fresh water. Tiani even bragged that she'd remembered to have the water purified by the scientists so that Levi wouldn't get sick.

Levi would eventually need to drink small amounts of water from the cenote to gradually build up an immunity to the microorganisms in order to live here long-term but not during their honeymoon.

When she had completed her tour of the one-room cottage, Levi realized this little space was just for them, a honeymoon suite designed for isolation. The thought reminded him the reason they were here, and again he was nervous.

"Would you like me to help you with your braids?" Levi asked Tiani, stepping closer to her and lifting the longest and thickest braid, which hung to the middle of her back. Just touching her for the first time was enough to send his heart and body into overdrive. The honor of using his fingers to comb through the interwoven locks of her hair was a sweet bonus for this night.

He took his time, unwinding each part slowly, then moving on to the next braid, gradually making his way around her head, letting the thick, brown locks fall across her shoulders and neck. When he turned her around and gazed upon her with her hair down for the first time, his breath caught. A sweet innocence replaced the stoic facade Tiani conveyed to everyone else. The soft smile on her face was reserved for him and him alone.

Without another word, Levi stepped closer and lifted her hair off her shoulders, letting the silken waves hang down her back. Then he leaned forward and kissed the right side of her neck, just behind her ear. A soft moan escaped her throat as he moved to the opposite side and kissed her there as well.

Kissing was a unique concept. Lips were such a sensitive collection of nerve endings that the mere act of pressing his lips to her body, anywhere on her body, elicited a reaction that flowed through him from the top of his head down to his toes.

The sleeves on the elegant wedding gown of silk and linen slipped easily over her shoulders. As Levi continued his path of kisses, Tiani reached for the buttons of his shirt, unbuttoning one at a time until his chest was exposed. She pulled the unnecessary article of clothing down and off, and it landed in a heap on the floor.

That simple act of his shirt hitting the floor at his feet was like permission to remove all other hindrances until they were skin to skin and pulling each other toward the bed. Joining himself in marriage, body and soul, with Tiani was the greatest experience of Levi's thirty years on earth.

Now Levi understood what Nicholas had meant when he'd said there was nothing in the world better than this.

Chapter Forty

Guatemala City

After one night at the hotel on the island in Flores, they had seen their parents safely onto an airplane before the twins and their wives took a private jet to Guatemala City.

The private jet was not fun. Tiani ended up panicking and needed a sedative shortly after takeoff along with a nap in the back bedroom of the jet. Levi held her as she clung to him in fear and whimpered every time they hit a patch of turbulence. Finally, she fell asleep and stayed asleep through the remainder of the flight to Guatemala City.

They were there to visit the office of the National Registry of Persons and get the process started which would establish Tiani as a person of record in the Republic of Guatemala. Having been born in the jungle village to a midwife, she, and everyone else in the village, had no record of having been born. This was common in Guatemala since there were so many indigenous tribes living in isolation spread out in the jungles. There was no need for a record unless someone planned to travel to another country, and Levi had promised to take Tiani to his village in Cambridge, Massachusetts.

Guatemala City was massive compared to anything Tiani had ever seen, and she was quickly overwhelmed. Levi tucked her protectively under his arm and led her to the places she needed to go. This was a complete role reversal from the confident tribal leader who guided the American scientists through the dense jungles around the temple pyramid. Levi worried how Tiani would handle the United States.

She'd been confused by the hotel with its hallways, indoor outhouse, running water, and televisions. Just as when she'd seen the computer for the first time, she tried to look behind the box to figure out where the picture and sound were coming from.

Tiani wasn't thrilled with the idea of someone *taking* her photograph. But when Levi explained that this was the only way she would be allowed to travel with him to see his village, she reluctantly agreed. Not until after Levi demonstrated the process.

Levi sat in the proffered chair at the photography studio and smiled, waiting for the telltale flash, and then he relaxed. The photographer invited them to come around behind the camera to see Levi's image on the digital screen. This helped Tiani understand that no one was actually taking something from her.

She still didn't understand how the face got on the screen like magic, but she allowed Levi to guide her to the chair.

Levi backed up and stood near the cameraman, making funny faces at Tiani until she smiled. This felt like working with a baby, but they eventually obtained a digital image that was acceptable for an identification and passport.

This was one of the last hoops to jump through while honeymooning in Guatemala City. The final printed documents, plus her newly created birth certificate, would be mailed to the base camp in Flores where they would wait to be picked up prior to flying to the States.

While he and Tiani were working with the government to prove she existed, Levi sent Nicholas and Becky on a quest to find a bookstore or a teacher's supply store to purchase instruction books on reading and writing Spanish and English, along with writing materials and a few simple books.

In his spare time, Levi planned to teach the people of the tribe how to read and write. They already knew how to speak and understand Spanish, and others besides Tiani had expressed interest in learning English. The instruction would be quite different from teaching a lecture hall full of college kids, but at least Levi knew how to teach. Very few tribes in the remote jungles of Guatemala would have the benefit of an American professor moving into their village.

On their second night at the hotel in Guatemala City, Levi almost couldn't get Tiani to come to bed because she was so fascinated with the books Nicholas and Becky had found. She was like a sponge soaking up all the knowledge she could.

Levi promised to teach Tiani more in the morning and enticed her with kisses, tempting her with the one desire she craved even more than knowledge. The one thing Levi craved more than anything else in the world.

Chapter Forty-One

Cacao Butter

L evi awoke with sunlight beaming through his window and the shower steaming up his attached bathroom. That alone was disorienting and a reminder he was home in Cambridge, Massachusetts after six weeks in the jungle.

What started as an archaeology exploration had shifted into an adventure that changed many lives, none more than the woman who had flown home with Levi and was enjoying a luxury unlike anything she'd known growing up.

Tiani had been introduced to modern facilities when they'd traveled to Guatemala City and was particularly fond of hot showers.

Levi pushed the sheets and blankets off and decided to join her. He'd never done anything so brazen. Although they'd been married over a month, most of their intimacy had happened late at night and in the dark.

Tiani was still somewhat shy with her body. Neither of them ever walked around their bedroom without clothes nor had they ever taken the time to really look at each other in broad daylight. There was something incredibly vulnerable about standing before someone else with nothing to hide every imperfection. Levi couldn't find anything imperfect about Tiani's body.

"Can I join you?" he asked in Yucatec, giving her the choice whether or not to invite him beyond the shower curtain that protected her privacy.

"Umm..." After a few seconds of hesitation, Tiani pulled the shower curtain to the side just far enough for him to step in next to her.

He tried very hard not to allow his eyes to wander even though that is exactly what he wanted to do. He locked her gaze and whispered, "Good morning." Her returning smile helped him to relax.

"You have no cacao butter for my hair."

That was the last thing Levi expected Tiani to say. He glanced at the synthetic shampoo and bodywash sitting next to a bar of generic deodorant soap he'd picked up at the grocery store and realized she had a valid complaint. "We can try to find a natural health store here in town. We need to go grocery shopping anyway."

"I don't know what that means." Her brow creased.

"Like a trading post, kind of like the ones near Tikal. We have stores here where we can buy food that we can't grow ourselves." This was a very strange conversation to have standing naked in the shower.

"Why can't you grow food?" Tiani didn't seem at all affected or bashful standing there with him. Maybe he'd been incorrect about her shyness.

"Because we live in a city. We hire farmers to grow food and bring the food to us here in the city. We trade money for food the same way you trade fruits and vegetables you grow for woven textiles to make your clothes." It occurred to Levi that they should probably shop for clothes for Tiani so she could feel comfortable while here in the States. "We can also go to a store and buy you some new clothes."

"Why do I need new clothes?" Her hands rested on his chest and Levi was momentarily tongue-tied, trying to come up with an answer while his heart rate increased. She often placed her hands on his chest, and he wondered if there was something symbolic to the gesture. The first time she ever touched him was the day she placed her hands on his chest to demand he translate conversations better. He certainly wasn't going to complain. But he did need to answer her question.

"The days and nights here become very cold and the dresses you wear in the jungle will not protect you enough." Hopefully that was a reasonable explanation. He wished Becky were here to help them shop. Maybe his mom could come to visit. She was only a half hour away and would probably love the chance to spend the day pampering her new daughter-in-law. He would call her when they got out of the shower.

Considering they would soon run out of hot water, Levi squeezed shampoo from the bottle and quickly lathered his hair, then shifted her body to the side so that he could easily rinse. Before he had the chance to duck his head under the water, Tiani reached up to touch the lathered shampoo and brought her fingers to her nose, which she wrinkled in disgust. He didn't suggest they put any shampoo in her hair. They would find something natural with cacao butter or a similar essential oil. Yeah, he was really going to need his mom's help today.

After rinsing the shampoo, Levi grabbed his bar of deodorant soap and was reminded again how exposed he was. He shouldn't feel self-conscious in front of his own wife, but he'd never taken a shower with another person. Maybe when he was a little boy and their mom had plopped Nicholas and him in the bath together, but not as an adult and definitely not with a woman.

Tiani seemed fascinated by the bar of soap also, taking it from Levi's hands and giggling when it slipped and thumped to the floor of the shower. She crouched down to pick up the bar, and it slipped through her fingers two more times before she captured it triumphantly with both hands. Trying to stand without the use of her hands, she looked up and Levi realized she was eye level with body parts he wouldn't show on the beach. Awkward.

Levi crouched down beside her and helped her to her feet, never offering any acknowledgement how close she'd been to parts he wasn't comfortable washing in front of her. Maybe this shower wasn't the best idea.

Until Tiani took the soap and rubbed it across his chest the same way he'd rubbed the soap down his arms. Okay, this could get fun.

Not wasting the opportunity, Levi reached for the poof sponge he had hanging from the showerhead and squirted some bodywash on, creating a sudsy, playful assortment of scented bubbles. He took the bar of soap and placed it back in the soap dish, then gently turned Tiani around to scrub the poof across her back.

A little whimper came from somewhere inside his wife, and Levi knew he was on the right track toward steering the conversation away from shopping excursions and essential oils to more interesting activities.

When he finished with her back and arms and neck, the next logical body parts were those that were more intimate. With barely a hesitation he continued, and she rested her back against his chest, eyes closed in blissful innocence and abandon.

He loved this woman for her spunk and fire and feistiness, as well as her inner beauty. At the time he married her, he never dreamed her body would be this incredible. Everything about her triggered physical reactions in his body that seemed insatiable. Thankfully Tiani seemed to react the same way to his body, and they connected like a two-piece jigsaw puzzle that was only whole when pieced together.

After scrubbing each other and rinsing each other and scrubbing and rinsing some more, the water started losing heat, and Levi turned off the shower and reached for a large, fluffy towel. He wrapped his wife in softness before carrying her to their bed. Shopping could wait a few hours. Maybe a few days.

Chapter Forty-Two

Omelets with Mom

Levi's doorbell rang almost simultaneously with his cell phone vibrating on the bedside table.

"What the heck?" Levi must have fallen back to sleep. They could blame jet lag or just the complete disregard for the need to rejoin society. Ten o'clock. Mid-morning. Who would be ringing his doorbell? The caller ID read Emilie Stephenson. He answered with mild disorientation. "Mom?"

"Come answer the door for your mother." Her voice didn't sound angry, more like excited.

Levi cleared his throat and glanced over at the angel beside him, whose eyes were barely opened. A sleepy smile was on her face. Sheets and blankets tangled his legs with hers, joining them, even in sleep. A wet towel lay on the floor beside the bed and Tiani's hair was strings of matted tangles. Oops. "I'm without apparel at the moment."

"Well, get out of bed and put some clothes on," his mom said. "I want to see my daughter-in-law."

"Only her?" Levi leaned down to kiss Tiani's lips before untangling himself from her and sliding to the edge of the bed. "Didn't miss your son at all?"

"Oh, phooey, I've known *you* all your life. I want to spend time with Tiani."

"I was actually going to call you today." Levi set the phone beside himself and turned on the speakerphone so he could dig through his drawer for a pair of sweats and a T-shirt. He found his smallest pair of workout shorts and handed them to Tiani, along with the smallest T-shirt he owned. "We need your help shopping."

"Ooh! I love shopping. Now come open the door."

"Unless you want to see parts of me you haven't seen since you stopped changing my diapers, you'll have to wait a minute." He stopped speaking English for a moment and spoke to Tiani in Yucatec. "My mom is here and wants to take us shopping. You can wear my clothes for a few minutes if you want."

Tiani picked up the shorts and T-shirt and brought them to her face, closing her eyes as she inhaled deeply. She pulled them under the covers with her and snuggled into the pillow, holding them like a security blanket.

"You keep that up, and we'll never make it to the store." Levi leaned closer, and she giggled, trying to pull him back down onto the bed. He resisted. Barely. "I have to go let my mother in the door. You get dressed, young lady."

"Do I have to?" Tiani pouted.

"I'm sure my mother doesn't want to see you naked any more than she wants to see me naked."

"You're no fun." She finally sat up, and Levi was distracted again by her upper half now completely exposed. He whimpered and almost told his mom to come back in an hour.

"We can have fun later." He leaned closer and gave her one more lingering kiss, forgetting he was still on the speakerphone.

"Levi Stephenson, stop making out with your wife and come open the door for your mother."

Levi groaned and pulled himself off the bed. He slipped on a pair of sweats and brought his shirt with him. To give Tiani a bit of privacy while she got dressed, he pulled the bedroom door shut and then headed down the stairs to open the front door.

"Good morning, Mother," Levi said, opening the door and ending the call in one sweeping motion.

"You're not even dressed yet." His mom pushed past him, entering the living room as if she owned the condo. "Put a shirt on. Where's my daughter-in-law?"

"In bed," Levi told her. "Where I should be. Also not dressed. Again, which I should be."

"Oh, give me a break," she said. "You've been married over a month. Don't you think it's time you came up for air?"

"No." Levi reluctantly slipped a shirt over his head.

"I brought food." She held up a grocery sack. "I figured you probably didn't have any groceries in the house after being gone all winter. I can cook us some omelets." She started opening cabinets and drawers to find the tools she needed, and Levi's stomach growled as if on cue.

"Oh, thank goodness," Levi said. "I'm starving. The last time I ate was dinner on the plane yesterday."

"Well, airplane food is barely considered food," she said. "That's not enough to sustain a growing boy."

"Mom, I'm thirty, and we took a private jet with a catering chef on board. I think I'll live." He pulled up a stool and watched his mother pull out all the things she needed and began cracking eggs into a bowl. "We need your help. Tiani needs clothes and something called cacao butter for her hair. Plus, whatever else women need. I'm clueless."

Tiani came down the stairs, hesitantly entering the kitchen and crossing the room to where Levi sat. He pulled her into his arms and had to remind himself that his mother was visiting.

"Oh! Sweetie, what happened to your hair?" His mom abandoned her workstation and pulled Tiani from Levi's arms, lifting the snarled masses off her shoulders as if picking up the pieces of a broken China doll. "You poor thing."

"Told you we need your help," Levi said.

"You should have called me sooner," she scolded her son.

"Trust me, you would not have wanted to be here any sooner this morning. There are reasons why her hair is a snarled mess and those reasons are not politely discussed in mixed company."

"You're insufferable."

"I'm in love." Levi sighed and held Tiani's gaze. She was too enamored to ask him to translate, but he switched to Yucatec anyway. "My mom's going to help you with your hair."

"Oh, thank goodness," Tiani said in Yucatec, then turned to her mother-in-law, switching to Spanish. "Gracias."

"I think I have a comb in my purse that we can use this morning and then buy one for you at the store later." She continued lifting matted strands of hair from Tiani's shoulders, smiling at her and completely forgetting she was supposed to speak in Spanish.

He realized that the entire conversation had been in English. "Mom, do you know how to speak Spanish?"

"Oh course," she said. "I was a refugee social worker in Belize for years." She seemed to realize her mistake and shifted to Spanish, apologizing to Tiani. Levi wondered how many times he'd need to remind her.

He redirected her attention back to the task at hand, cooking breakfast. "Can we eat first?" Levi asked. "Your son is starving, remember?"

"How about if *you* make the omelets," his mom said. "And I'll spend time with this beautiful wife of yours?"

"Unless you want a frozen meal warmed up in the microwave or a protein shake, you might want to do the cooking yourself," Levi said. "Please, Mommy?"

"Oh, so I'm Mommy again when you want food." She laughed. "I see how you are."

Levi pulled Tiani away and pointed his mom toward the kitchen counter where she was chopping green peppers and onions.

Levi saw a loaf of bread in the grocery sack, which was now tipped on its side, exposing the contents. He lifted Tiani onto the stool where he'd been sitting and crossed the room to start some toast. His mom had even remembered to bring butter and jelly. Pulling glasses from the cabinet, he poured some juice for each of them, then set the table with plates and napkins and forks.

Tiani was his mom's captive audience, watching as she poured the beaten eggs into the heated pan as the butter sizzled along the edges.

Like an expert chef, his mom lifted the sides of the omelet, letting the uncooked egg flow down and around the outside, and then moved on to the next side, then the next. The result was a fluffy cloud of egg that she flipped with a twitch of her wrist. She sprinkled shredded cheddar onto the eggs, added the chopped onions and peppers, and folded one half over the other.

Just as she slipped the masterpiece onto a platter, the toast popped, and Levi lifted each piece from the toaster and spread butter over the crispy bread and then a thin layer of jelly. He took a plate from the cupboard, added a slice of toast and a portion of the omelet, and then set them on the table along with a glass of juice.

Holding out his hand to help Tiani off the stool, he guided her over to the table and held out the chair for her. His mom prepared the other two plates and Levi helped carry them to the table before sitting beside his wife.

Before taking her seat, his mom reached into her purse and pulled out a scrunchie. She stood behind Tiani and gathered her hair back to keep it from getting in her food.

Tiani leaned her head back to look up at her mother-in-law and thanked her, then picked up her fork and took a bite of the omelet. She stopped chewing a second, and Levi was afraid she was going to spit it back out and say she didn't like it. Instead she moaned and said in Yucatec, "This is so good!"

Levi turned to his mom. "She loves it."

"Oh, good! I'm so glad." His mom clapped her hands together once, then forgetting herself, repeated the sentiment in Spanish.

Realizing her mistake as well, Tiani repeated her compliment in Spanish.

And just like that, his mom and Tiani were new besties.

Chapter Forty-Three

Fixing the Mess You Made

"**O**kay, hold still and I'll try to get some of these tangles out without hurting you too badly." Levi's mom had Tiani sitting on the stool in the kitchen, a large-toothed comb in her hand, working her way up and down the snarled mess. There were good reasons why Tiani always wore her hair braided and this was one of them.

Levi loaded the dishwasher, wiped the counters, cleared the table, and put all the leftover food in the refrigerator. Seeing they didn't need him for anything else, Levi hitched his thumb over his shoulder. "I'm going to try again to take a shower... without the distraction this time."

"Is *that* what caused this rat's nest?" His mom's eyes gleamed with understanding.

"I don't know." Levi sighed and leaned closer to kiss Tiani's lips before heading upstairs. "It was all kind of a blur. And then I fell asleep."

Tiani giggled and pushed him away. "Go take a shower. Don't bother us. Your mom's trying to fix the mess you made."

"As you wish, Your Highness." Levi bowed regally to his princess and climbed the stairs to his room, his hunger for breakfast the only need completely satisfied.

By the time Levi returned to the kitchen, his mom was just finishing an elegant braid that wrapped all the way around Tiani's head like a crown.

"Oh, wow, you look elegant," Levi said in Yucatec, his words laced with awe. Then he switched to Spanish. "Mom, you're a miracle worker. Where did you learn to do that? You don't even have any daughters."

She smiled wistfully, pulling together the final touches. "When I helped with the refugees, the children often arrived with matted, snarled messes, and they loved to have someone pamper them a little, cleaning off the dust and grime, washing their hair, combing out the tangles. And braids. Every little girl needs braids. Whenever I would wrap their little heads in a braided crown, they felt like princesses." She leaned around and smiled at her daughter-in-law. "Do you feel like a princess now?"

"Mom, she *is* a princess," Levi said.

"But now I *feel* like a princess." Tiani rose from the stool and wrapped her arms around her mother-in-law. She whispered close to her ear. "Thank you for giving me your son."

"You're welcome, sweetheart."

This was a far cry from the woman who all but demanded Levi not marry Tiani. All his mom needed was to meet this woman to agree she was captivating.

"Now, go get dressed so we can do some shopping."

"You need any help?" Levi asked Tiani, baiting his mom.

"*You* stay here." His mom grabbed his arm. "You are the opposite of help. We'll never get to the shopping mall if you keep that up."

Within two minutes of Tiani walking up the stairs, she called down to him. "Levi, I have a problem."

He took the stairs two at a time and found her standing in the middle of their bedroom, holding two very threadbare and filthy dresses. They'd looked beautiful while amongst the other villagers in the jungle, but they would never do for Cambridge, Massachusetts.

"I need new clothes." Her shoulders slumped.

"Yes, you do." He came to her and pulled both dresses from her hands and draped them over his arm. "I will put these in the washing machine, and you can stay in those jogging shorts for now. The first place we'll shop will be a clothing department store, and when you leave that store, you'll be wearing something almost as beautiful as you."

She followed him back down the stairs, still wearing a T-shirt and shorts, and slipped into her laced moccasins. "This looks ridiculous."

"We'll buy you some shoes also."

"I have my gym clothes in the car," his mom exclaimed. "Tiani will probably fit better into *my* jogging pants than yours. Plus, my sneakers are in there." Without another word, his mom hurried out the door and down the porch steps to her car, returning with a gym bag filled with women's clothes.

"Perfect," Levi said.

"Thank you so much." Tiani clutched the clothes to her chest the way she'd done with his T-shirt and shorts, minus the deep breath to treasure the fragrance of Levi's cologne. He couldn't imagine his mom's clothes smelled quite as good after being in the trunk of her car.

Tiani hurried up the stairs with her treasures and came down a few minutes later with a smile. She was an entirely different person than he'd met six weeks ago. The cold, aloof mask of royalty had been stripped away to reveal a happy, shining beacon of love. Maybe that was just his perception. Whichever part she played, the Mayan princess and daughter of the chief or the playful woman who shared his bed, he loved them all.

As Tiani laced up the shoes, which were a half size too large, his mom dug her keys from her purse.

"I'll drive," his mom said. "Tiani can sit up front with me, and you can sit in the back and tell us where to go."

"Easy," Levi said. "The Prudential Center. That's where all the upscale department stores are."

"Sweetie, she's not going to feel comfortable going there in sweatpants and oversized shoes." Levi's mom glanced at him in the rearview mirror with a condescending raise of her eyebrows. "Let's try something... less... upscale."

"Okay, let me do a little Googling." Levi pulled out his smartphone and searched for clothing stores, which brought up three-hundred choices. Wondering how best to narrow the search he typed in "ethnic clothing" and up popped a boutique selling Peruvian clothing. Perfect. Clothes made in South America. Can't get any better than that. The Incans were often compared to the Mayans. He requested directions from Google Maps, and they were on their way.

Ten minutes later, they walked into the most elegant collection of women's clothing Levi had ever seen. The place even smelled authentic.

A rather uppity salesclerk approached them. "Buenos días, how may I help you?"

Tiani jumped on the chance to communicate in Spanish and told the woman she needed to buy some clothing.

"I... don't speak much Spanish," the woman said.

Tiani turned to Levi, frustrated that the woman was speaking English. Skipping back to her native tongue, Tiani spoke in Yucatec. "What is she saying?"

"She said she doesn't know how to speak Spanish," Levi answered in Yucatec.

"Then why did she address us in Spanish?"

"I think she was being snooty," Levi said, not sure if the word he used in Yucatec was even close to the message he was trying to convey. "I have an idea. Play up the confident tribal princess thing, and I'll translate for you. Sound good?"

Tiani lifted her chin in the air and said in her most aloof manner. "That will be acceptable." Perfect.

Levi winked at Tiani and turned to the salesclerk again. "Her Highness was confused why you addressed her in Spanish if you don't speak the language."

"I'm very sorry. I didn't mean to offend you... or her... uh, what language were you just speaking? That didn't sound like Spanish."

"We were speaking Yucatec, one of the Mayan languages the princess uses among her tribal members."

"Are *you* one of her tribal members? You spoke that language perfectly."

"No, I am her husband. Her Highness has given me permission to translate so that you can help her replace the wardrobe that didn't make it onto our private jet when we left Guatemala yesterday. Would you be available to assist her? She will feel much more comfortable when she is clothed in proper attire."

"Of course." The woman gulped and stuttered. "I'll be more than happy to assist... uh... the princess."

"Allow me to introduce Her Highness, Princess Tiani Sayid, daughter of Prince Gabor Sayid from the Republic of Guatemala."

"It's a pleasure to meet you, Your Highness." The salesclerk held out her hand but Tiani glanced down her nose with disdain.

"It is not customary for people to shake hands in her culture nor would she... since you are beneath her in stature and lineage. Could you please direct us to something more fitting than my mother's gym clothes?"

The woman pulled her hand back and lifted her chin. "Of course. Right this way." She turned and headed toward the back where more high-end clothing hung from racks.

Over the next two hours, Tiani enjoyed the pampering that only comes to the uber-rich and royalty, both of which she was. Once she tried on the first classy Pima jacquard dress and slipped on a pair of matching heels, she transformed before their eyes from a dowdy little girl to an elegant woman.

She didn't bother with Spanish for the remainder of the excursion, choosing instead to continue the haughty facade of exclusivity that comes with speaking a language no one else understands. His mother hung back, knowingly grinning as she chose dresses and slacks and tops she thought Tiani might like.

As much as Levi wanted to snub this woman who had spoken rudely when they arrived, he wanted to please his wife even more. The salesclerk earned her commission check, and by the time they were done shopping, her commission would likely feed her family for a month.

Levi carried bags of clothing to the trunk of his mother's car, then took Tiani's hand to help her into the front seat.

Now she was ready for upscale shopping at The Prudential Center.

Levi hoped finding cacao butter would be that easy.

Chapter Forty-Four

Dress Shopping

Before heading to Boston to shop at The Prudential Center, Levi did a little more research on his smartphone and found a local health food store that sold cacao butter and other products containing cacao butter.

The clerk at Cambridge Naturals was very helpful and talked with Tiani in broken Spanish, with Levi and his mom translating when needed. Tiani walked away with several hundred dollars' worth of all-natural skin and hair products. Levi was excited to try some of them, now that they both realized how much fun showering together could be.

When they arrived at The Prudential Center, they decided they were ready for lunch and chose an upscale restaurant. Levi helped Tiani choose a meal based on a few questions about meats and vegetables and breads. In the end, they settled on a filet mignon with sautéed asparagus and roasted potatoes with soft garlic bread.

Levi ordered a grilled salmon steak with rice pilaf and almond green beans, and his mom chose a chicken breast drizzled with a creamy alfredo sauce and linguine so that Tiani could have a taste of a variety of foods.

Tiani loved everything, and Levi found she was easy to please with her culinary tastes, clothing choices, body care, and especially lovemaking. He started to wonder if there was anything about her that was not perfect.

After lunch, they found a women's clothing store where his mom and Tiani were able to find more intimate items such as bras and underwear. Levi wondered if she'd ever worn a bra before, but she seemed to like the feeling of support a bra provided.

His mom got so bold as to hold up a silk negligee she thought Levi might appreciate.

"Thank you, Mother. That will look very nice lying on the floor next to our bed."

"Good point." She shoved the hanger back in among the other useless articles of clothing.

"How about some soft pajamas she could wear to lounge around the house?" Levi suggested. "Also, maybe some yoga pants and hoodies and comfortable shirts? We've bought everything needed for more formal public outings but nothing for comfort at home."

"Not *every* formal public outing..." His mom hesitated and sized Tiani up as if she were a model. "Have you thought about what she will wear to your brother's wedding?"

"No..." Levi pursed his lips. "What would you suggest?"

Tiani just stood there looking back and forth between them.

"How about a traditional Guatemalan wedding dress?" his mom suggested.

"Mom, it's not *our* wedding. The day is to celebrate Nicholas and Becky. We don't want to upstage Becky's special day."

"Why not?" His mom lifted her chin. "This is the first time your family will meet *your* bride as well. Can't she look the part?"

"Our family will be glad to meet her, but I doubt Becky's family would appreciate us showing up looking like it's a double wedding."

"Well, maybe something formal and Guatemalan but not too ostentatious." She stepped over to Tiani and lifted her chin in the loving way a mother would scrutinize her elegant daughter. "This princess deserves something special."

"Thank you." Tiani lowered her eyes, bashful from the praise.

They finished with the casual shopping and headed upstairs to a specialty bridal and formalwear store where the saleswoman took Tiani under her wing, offering to create a masterpiece for the princess. As wonderful as that sounded, there were only a few days left before they had to leave for Texas.

The saleswoman found a royal purple Magdalena satin ball gown, which she dressed up with a semi-transparent silk shawl in a complimentary fuchsia. The look was just elegant enough to pass as a bridal gown, had it been white.

"It's perfect," Levi said reverently, then switched to Yucatec to offer a compliment meant to be shared between the two of them. "You look elegant, my princess. I wish you could wear your crown. The feathers would match those colors."

"What if we carefully removed the feathers from my crown and wove them into a braided crown similar to the style your mother created this morning?" Tiani and Levi met each other's eyes in the three-way mirror of the upscale formalwear store, then both scrutinized the braid as if envisioning the results.

"That sounds beautiful, my love." Still speaking Yucatec, Levi carefully wrapped his arms around her waist and pulled her just a little closer. "I have found you beautiful from the moment we met, and you have been, and will always be, most beautiful in your traditional clothing, but your elegance is going to steal the spotlight in this gown."

"Do you think I shouldn't wear the gown?" She bit her lower lip.

"No, I think you *should* wear the gown," Levi whispered even though no one else could understand them while speaking her native language. "You are royalty and will be on the arm of one of the richest men in the room. I want you to own that position."

"If you're by my side, I'll be the richest woman in the room," she whispered back.

They leaned closer to one another and shared a mildly passionate kiss that probably made the others in the room uncomfortable.

When they finally pulled apart, Levi pressed his forehead to hers and whispered again, "Let's go home and try out some of those new bath oils."

Tiani giggled in answer, and Levi turned to the saleswoman.

"We'll take the dress."

Chapter Forty-Five

Don't Hurt My Car

"Today, I want to take you over to my office and show you off to my colleagues."

"I don't know what that means." Tiani rolled over in bed and propped herself up on one elbow. They'd been awake for a little while just lying in bed, talking and kissing and goofing off. Eventually they'd need to get up and make some breakfast. Before they'd gone home the previous afternoon, they'd stopped by the grocery store and picked up some very basic foods since neither Tiani nor Levi had any real cooking skills.

"My office is the place where I work," Levi explained. Not everything translated perfectly to Yucatec. Plus, people didn't have jobs in the tribal village like Americans did. They all just sort of helped each other. Hunting, farming, cooking, gathering wild fruits, nuts, fibrous plants, scouting for dangers, basically protecting themselves and the temple pyramid. "My colleagues are the people I work with."

"Okay, whatever you say. I will follow you and you can—how did you say—show me off."

"You will like my books," Levi said. He pictured all the shelves filled with ancient and modern languages, symbology, translations, photographs of archeological sites.

"You have books?" Tiani sat up, excited. She'd been fascinated with the books they bought in Guatemala City, and he wanted to purchase more books and writing materials and instruction aides. If he was going to be spending time in the village, he needed to be contributing something and teaching languages was what he was good at. "Can we leave right now?"

"Sure. I need a shower and some breakfast, but then we can leave."

They hurried through morning preparations for the day, then headed down to the garage where they had a dilemma.

"I've never driven this car before..." He stood beside Tiani, both staring at the candy-apple-red luxury SUV with its $270,000 valuation and nervously remembered the words Nicholas had said to him over and over: don't touch my car. "Can't be much different than any other car, right?"

"I don't know what that means," Tiani said in Yucatec. She'd only sat in a car a few dozen times in her life.

"Of course not," Levi grumbled. He held open the passenger side door and helped her inside. He walked around the front. "I may need to call my brother."

Levi realized he hadn't called Nicholas since he and Tiani arrived at the condo. That had been the first night that he and Nicholas had slept in a different town, a different state, on opposite sides of the country. If he hadn't had Tiani by his side, he might have spiraled into depression and anxiety.

Staying in a hotel or tent with Nicholas on the other side of a wall had been easy. Giving Tiani a grand tour of his condo was difficult. This is Nicholas's bedroom. This is Nicholas's home office. This is Nicholas's computer workstation and collection of books and maps and charts. This is Nicholas's car. We'll drive it to Houston for him in a few days. I'll spend the night in the same city as my twin in just a few days.

Levi shook off the despair and pulled out his cellphone.

Nicholas answered on the first ring. "Miss me already, little brother?"

"Not nearly as soon as I thought I would." Levi chuckled and slipped into the fine leather driver's seat. "But we've been a little busy so there hasn't been much time to miss you."

"Yeah, Mom told me how she walked in on you two."

"She did *not* walk in on us," Levi corrected his twin. "The front door was locked, and we had recently fallen asleep... without clothing. Plus, I may or may not have caused a complete rat's nest in my wife's hair after our shower."

"*Our* shower?" Nicholas laughed. "Sounds like fun. May have to try that later with Becky."

"Yeah, not all of us have a cenote tucked into our backyard," Levi said, then glanced over at Tiani, realizing the whole conversation had been in

English other than the word cenote. He knew he should switch to Spanish but wanted to get driving instructions in English.

"You will when you return to your wife's native village."

"That's almost an incentive to pack my bags right now and order the private jet to take us home." Levi winked at Tiani even though she likely had no idea what he was saying.

"Not until after my wedding, dude."

"I wouldn't miss it for the world," Levi said. "But first, please tell me how to start the engine on your Lamborghini."

"Dude, don't touch my car, man."

"Dude, when did you take up surfing?" Levi asked. "This is the only car we own, and I need to know how to drive the beast so I can bring it to you when we drive to Houston. Now tell me how to turn the dang thing on."

"There's a little red latch up by the cup holders." Nicholas almost sounded as if he was speaking through clenched teeth. "Open the latch and push the button that says 'start'. This shouldn't be that difficult."

"Any tips for driving the thing?"

"Yeah, keep it in strada mode. It's designed for everyday use. The ride will be so smooth you'll feel like you're driving a Lexus."

"I've never driven a Lexus, so that's not a good comparison, but I'll take your word for it. Wow, it's so quiet." Just as he commented on the sound of the engine, the Bluetooth hooked the car to his cell phone and Nicholas's voice boomed into the cab, startling Tiani.

"Where are you taking my baby, anyway?" Nicholas asked.

"This morning, we are going to campus so I can show off my elegant wife. No one is going to believe the geek twins went away for the winter and came back married. What are the odds?"

"Apparently in our favor," Nicholas said.

"Okay, how do you get this thing in reverse?" Levi asked, looking around for some sort of gear shift.

"There's a lever right above the start button. Pull that back. Then the other shifting paddles are on the steering wheel."

"Weird, but okay." Levi pulled back the lever and eased his foot off the brake, allowing the car to slowly reverse out of the garage. "Okay, I need to focus on driving now. I'll call if I need any more help."

"Be careful, please," Nicholas said.

"Eh, don't worry about us." Levi said, looking over his shoulder as he backed up. "This baby has three-sixty airbags. We will most likely live through a crash."

"I meant be careful of my car." Nicholas sounded as if he was growling.

"Oh, right, I knew what you meant," Levi teased. "I'll be sure to park her in a nice, tight space between two college students with beaters."

"You'd better not!"

"You're so gullible," Levi said. "Goodbye."

"Goodbye."

Levi shifted into drive and barely touched the accelerator before they were already flying down the road.

Chapter Forty-Six

Honored to Meet You

"**D**r. Stephenson, welcome home. How was your expedition this winter?" Dr. Larry Ives thrust his hand forward in greeting, then seemed to notice Tiani for the first time. "Well, well, well, who do we have here?"

Levi didn't like the way his colleague was leering at Tiani. He knew she was beautiful, and everywhere they went men would find her attractive, but he needed to put a stop to this now.

"Dr. Ives, allow me to introduce my *wife*, Tiani Sayid." Levi placed a hand on Tiani's back as if displaying her.

"Good morning, Tiani," Dr. Ives said, redirecting his hand of greeting. His words were slick, like a used car salesman. Levi had never really liked Dr. Ives. He was a relatively new faculty member who taught entry level theory of archeology. A classic example of the cliché mantra about those who cannot do, teach. "Pleasure to meet you."

Tiani didn't answer, nor did she reach forward to shake his hand, but merely raised her chin in the air and glanced at Levi, waiting for him to intervene on her behalf.

Not wanting to hide a word of what he was about to say, Levi asked Dr. Ives if he spoke Spanish.

"Uh, yes," Dr. Ives said in Spanish. "A little."

Levi immediately switched to Spanish, talking slowly to accommodate Dr. Ives's limitations. "It is not customary to shake one another's hand in my wife's culture, nor *would* she shake your hand, seeing as how you are beneath her in stature and lineage."

"Huh?" Dr. Ives said, dropping his hand to his side. He switched to English. "I understood very little of that. Something about my hand and your wife."

Before Levi translated for his colleague, he turned to Tiani and spoke in Yucatec. "He doesn't understand Spanish well, so I'm going to repeat what I just said in English for his benefit."

"That will be acceptable," Tiani said, also in Yucatec, once again playing the part he'd coached her to play. She seemed to be having fun with this.

"My wife is the daughter of her tribal chief and a princess in the Sayid royal family; therefore, it would be considered beneath her to shake your hand," Levi said in English. "It is also not customary to shake one another's hand in her Mayan culture."

"Okay, wait. Back up. What language were you just speaking?"

"Yucatec," Levi said. "My wife's native language."

"When did you get married?" Dr. Ives creased his brow. "And... how many languages do you speak?"

"Fluently? Let me think." Levi turned to Tiani and asked in Yucatec, "How many days ago did we get married?"

"Thirty-two?" She guessed, cocking her head to the side. He decided to take her guess as accurate.

"We were wed thirty-two days ago," Levi said in English, turning back to his colleague, counting on his fingers. "And I am fluent in English, Spanish, French, German, Finnish, Swedish, Mandarin, Arabic, Hebrew, Hindi, and Portuguese. I know a little Swahili, but I haven't focused my studies on the African languages because there are almost two thousand of them. Plus, as long as you know Arabic, French, English, and Portuguese, that pretty much covers the ability to communicate with most people on the African continent. My *main* focus has been in the Mayan languages. I'm fluent in almost all ancient and modern languages of the Maya. How many was that? Were you counting? I ran out of fingers."

Dr. Ives stood there with his mouth gaping. He gulped and whispered, "I would have been impressed with four or five."

"There's a reason why I'm world-renowned in my field." Levi patted Dr. Ives on the arm and looked over his shoulder. "Oh, look, there's Dr. Sedwick. I wanted to introduce him to my wife. Nice talking with you, Dr. Ives."

"You too…" Dr. Ives's face was still creased in shock, and Levi wondered if he was still counting.

"What did you say to him?" Tiani whispered, even though no one else would understand her speaking Yucatec.

"I was just bragging a little." Levi kissed her on the cheek and then switched to English and called out to his department chairman. "Dr. Sedwick! I want to introduce you to my wife."

"Ah, the prodigal twin has returned to clean out his desk," Dr. Sedwick said, skipping the handshake and pulling Levi into a hug.

Levi froze. Had he been fired? He squeaked out a reply. "I'm just taking a sabbatical. Do I need to clean out my desk for that?"

"I thought you got married." Dr. Sedwick pulled back with a grin. "And here's your lovely bride. You met in Guatemala, right?" He must have realized that the Mayans didn't shake hands because instead he offered Tiani a slight bow of respect.

"Yes, this is Tiani Sayid," Levi said. "She only speaks Spanish and Yucatec. Do you speak either language?"

"Si, puedo hablar español," Dr. Sedwick said, acknowledging that he did indeed speak Spanish. The remainder of the introductions would be easier. He started by asking Tiani what she did for a living. She still didn't completely understand the concept of a person having a *job*, per se. Everyone in the tribe helped out wherever they were needed, and the tribe had most things in common. There was no need for money or riches.

"I am the daughter of Chief Gabor Sayid, and a tribal leader," Tiani said, repeating what Levi had taught her to say when people asked about her and what role she played in her community.

"You must miss your family, living here in the States," Dr. Sedwick said with an understanding tone.

"We've been too busy to miss my family." Tiani blushed and lowered her eyes. Levi knew exactly what she meant by "busy," and it had nothing to do with shopping trips and sightseeing.

"How long have you lived in the United States?" Dr. Sedwick asked. He seemed confused.

"Three days? Two days?" She glanced at Levi. "How long have we been here?"

"We got here three days ago," Levi said. "So, two nights. But we'll probably live here half the year and go home to Guatemala the other half the year."

"I thought she lived in Houston," Dr. Sedwick said, cocking his head to the side.

"You think I'm Nicholas, don't you?" Understanding came over Levi. "I'm Levi."

"Levi? But I thought Nicholas was the one who got married."

"We both did," Levi said with a smile. "Nicholas married Dr. Rebecca Benson from the University of Houston at the National Center for Airborne Laser Mapping. And I had the honor of marrying Princess Tiani Sayid of the Mayan tribe protecting the temple pyramid we discovered near Tikal using the new LiDAR technology." Levi stepped closer and wrapped his arm around Tiani's shoulders.

"No kidding? What a small and beautiful world we live in." Dr. Sedwick once again bowed his head. "I'm honored to meet you, Your Highness."

"Thank you," she said. "I'm honored to meet you as well."

"Did you know that you are married to one of the most talented linguists who ever walked the earth?"

"I understand he is talented at a great number of things."

Levi scratched his head and cleared his throat, humbled by their praise. "Anyway..."

Tiani and Dr. Sedwick both chuckled.

"I want to show Tiani my office, and then we plan to go shopping for books. Tiani and I will be helping teach her tribe to read and write Spanish and English."

"What a wonderful endeavor," Dr. Sedwick said. "Good luck with that. And for the record, I'm glad you're only taking a sabbatical. Didn't want to lose you both. Never thought I'd see the day when something would separate the geek twins."

"I never thought I'd see the day either," Levi said. "Good thing we have our wives to keep us... busy."

"Indeed." Dr. Sedwick inclined his head with a gleam in his eyes. "Have fun with your tour and book shopping. Let me know when you're ready to get back in the classroom."

"Probably fall semester," Levi said. "Although I'm not sure how well I'll handle the Guatemalan rainy season this summer."

"I don't think I could handle it either," Dr. Sedwick said, chuckling as he walked away. "Good luck with that."

When Levi turned back around after saying goodbye to his department chair, he caught a look of anger or confusion on Tiani's face. *Great. What had he done?*

Chapter Forty-Seven

My Place Is with You

"Hey, princess," Levi spoke softly in Yucatec. "You look upset."
After his department chair, Dr. Sedwick walked away, Tiani
pulled herself back into the mask she often maintained while serving
as a tribal leader. The mask he hadn't seen since they left Guatemala.

"I'm fine." She lifted her chin with a confidence that seemed fake.

If Levi had learned anything from his father, uncles, colleagues,
friends, basically any married man he'd ever met, it was that when your
wife says she's "fine" you can guarantee she's the opposite of fine, and
most likely whatever she's upset about is your fault.

"Show me this place of teaching you have." Her words were clipped,
confirming his fears. He tried to recap the most recent things he'd said
and done to figure out what had happened to upset her.

Levi knew Dr. Ives had been lewd, but Dr. Sedwick had been polite
and jovial. Was she upset with something he said? Or could something
he said have been misinterpreted? He'd complimented them on their
desire to teach the tribal members, told Levi he was glad they wouldn't
be losing him. Levi had mentioned he might want to return to the
classroom in the fall semester. That had to be it!

"Are you upset that I wanted to return to teach here in the fall?"

"Doesn't the rain ever come to your village?" Tiani stopped short
and pursed her lips.

"Yes, we have lots of rain here in Cambridge." Levi hesitated. Where
was she going with this?

"What is different about the rainy season in my village compared to
your village?"

Now he understood. Levi had told Dr. Sedwick he couldn't handle the Guatemalan rainy season. "Well, the main difference is the duration. In most parts of the United States, rain lasts a few hours, maybe a few days at most, and then the rain stops. In your village, the rain stays for months."

"Why did you agree to marry me if you can't handle the rain?"

"I love you. I will live wherever you want me to live. If you want to live in your village forevermore, I will move there today."

Her face softened. "You would do that?"

"Of course." He hadn't dared to reach out for her in fear she might pull away, but now he pulled her close. "I want to be where you are. My home is wherever you are. You are the most important person in my world." Levi hesitated. Was that true? Had he really just admitted that there was someone else more important than his twin?

A peace came over his heart. Yes. Tiani was more important than his twin. He would choose her over him. He *had* chosen her over him. Knowing Nicholas was only a phone call away and only a flight away made that choice easier, but Levi's place was with his wife. And Nicholas's place was with Becky. That's how marriage worked.

"My place is with you." Levi pulled her just a little closer for a soft kiss. Nothing inappropriate for the hallway at the university and nothing that conveyed the message let's go home and continue this conversation. Just a nice, sweet kiss to reassure his wife. He took a step back and met her gaze. "Are you ready to see all my books?"

Tiani relaxed and smiled lightly, then nodded her head. "Yes, show me your books."

The Tozzer Anthropology Building was a fascinating place for a person intrigued by archaeology and ancient structures. Levi brought Tiani into his office and pulled books with pictures and drawings of antiquities in ancient Mesoamerica from his shelves.

While Tiani sat at his desk, Levi brought her maps of the area showing where her village was located in relation to other places she knew, such as Tikal and Flores and Guatemala City.

He saw the moment her brain connected the dots and realized how big the world was beyond her little jungle forest. She knew there was a four-hour walk between her village and Tikal, and a one-hour drive between Tikal and Flores, and an airplane ride to Guatemala City. Those were all tiny dots on the map of her country, almost too small to be noticeable on the continent of Central America, and non-existent on a world map.

"I have a lot to learn," Tiani whispered in a shaky voice.

"You have a lifetime to learn it all." Levi wrapped his arms around her from behind, leaning over her and resting his chin on her shoulder.

"I don't think it's possible to learn it all." Her voice cracked as if she was getting emotional. "All this, and you still want to know what the writings mean on the temple? Why?"

"I'm not sure how to explain it." He tried to seriously consider her question. "Your people were smart—are still smart," he hurried to add.

Levi removed his arms from her shoulders and lowered himself to one knee beside her, realizing what he was about to tell her was probably going to be disorienting.

"A few hundred years ago, most of your people disappeared from the world very suddenly. Why? What happened that caused your people to disappear? Scientists hope that by studying what your people wrote and drew we could understand what happened."

"How many of my people were there?" Tiani gulped, vulnerability in her eyes.

"Millions."

"How many is that?" She pulled away just enough to meet his gaze.

"As many as the sands on the seashore."

"I don't know what that means." She shook her head, brows creased. He realized she had never been anywhere near an ocean. These concepts were beyond her limited understanding.

"I'll show you sometime." Levi leaned forward and kissed the tip of her nose.

"Okay." She turned back toward the desk and ran her hands over the beautiful atlas of the world with all its mystery.

"Let's go to the bookstore," Levi suggested. "We can find some books to take home with us and teach our people."

"Where is home, Levi?" she whispered.

"In our village in Guatemala." He placed a finger on the map right where he knew her village lay.

Tiani lifted his hand and splayed his fingers, then pressed his hand onto the page, covering most of Central America. She then moved his hand over the map of the world in a broad circle. "My home is wherever you are."

Chapter Forty-Eight

Meeting the Sayid Princes

Levi's father, Henry Stephenson, was a cousin to a man who happened to be best friends with one of the Sayid princes. With a few phone calls, Levi's Uncle Alex was able to arrange to have Tiani meet her distant cousins.

The three-hour drive from Cambridge to where the Sayid princes lived near Kingston, New York, was up and over and through hills and valleys and forests and supposedly ended at a place his Uncle Alex referred to as the tree house. Levi wasn't even sure who owned the house, just that it was the place they all met whenever there was a family gathering.

Tiani and Levi would be spending the night at the tree house, which apparently had to be seen to be understood.

Levi still felt a sense of melancholy from Tiani even though they had come to several understandings, the most important of which was that they were both willing to uproot their lives to be with each other. They also realized life wasn't going to be as easy as they'd like to imagine in their childish dreams of growing up and getting married and living happily ever after.

Tiani was frustrated about the language barrier and always needing to have translators. She was more determined than ever to learn English, but Levi could tell what she really wanted was to go home. She missed her parents, her friends, her simple life. She didn't have to play a role or pretend to be someone she wasn't. She knew her place. She wanted the comfort of normalcy.

After shopping at the university bookstore and bringing home stacks of books, most of them primers designed to help teachers teach basic

English and Spanish, she spread the books out on the kitchen table at their townhouse and immersed herself in learning.

Just as when they had stayed at the hotel in Guatemala City, Levi had to lure Tiani to bed with soft words, promising he'd teach her more tomorrow. Unlike the night in Guatemala City, she didn't turn to him for comfort. That was one of the first nights since they'd gotten married that they hadn't made love.

The only other time was when Tiani had claimed to have stomach pains and told Levi she wouldn't feel well for a few days, and she didn't want to talk about it. Although he'd never had sisters or a girlfriend, Levi had a basic understanding of women's monthly cycles and didn't want to talk about it anymore than Tiani did.

Now, he didn't even want to think those cliché words about the honeymoon being over. She was just homesick. He hoped the drive over to visit her distant cousins would help break up the overwhelming feeling of trying to assimilate into his world. Neither of them had ever met the princes so this would be new to both of them.

When the navigation system in the Lamborghini instructed them to turn right into a long driveway, it also told them they had arrived at their destination. Although hesitant, Levi took the car's word for it and crept down the tree-lined path into the woods, no apparent end in sight.

Tiani's eyes were alight with excitement at driving through the tunnel of trees. The driveway seemed to last forever until, finally, they came upon a house built up and around and practically *in* the trees.

Although Levi understood immediately why they called it a tree house, the most impressive feature about the house had nothing to do with the trees and everything to do with the waterfall that literally flowed under and through the foundation of the house. It was as if the designer had wanted the house to overlook the waterfall and be a part of the landscape. The combination was elegant and awe inspiring.

Before the car came to a complete stop, Levi's uncle Alex rolled to the edge of the driveway in his stylish wheelchair that looked almost impressive enough to be its own sports car.

Alexander Stephenson, Jr., who was Levi's father's cousin, had been in a tragic drunk driving accident in his senior year of high school that left him in a coma for three days and nearly paralyzed from the waist down. After months of physical therapy, he was able to stand briefly but had yet to walk.

He sure could talk though. Uncle Alex toured the world as a motivational speaker, inspiring a platform fighting teen drinking.

His best friend, Prince Augustus Sayid, the youngest of the Sayid princes, had been driving that night. Gus, and all three of his brothers, had been as inebriated as Uncle Alex and had driven his car into a telephone pole. They were all lucky to be alive, and the experience changed them. And changed the community forever.

"Dang! Where did you get this ride, little man?" Uncle Alex asked as Levi climbed from the Lamborghini. He'd always called both of the twins "little man" because he could never tell them apart.

"Nicholas found this at the Beijing Auto Show a few years back and slapped down the two-seventy to get the first run." Before stopping to shake his uncle's hand, Levi opened the passenger door for his bride, being sure to introduce Tiani first. Leading her from the car, he said, "Uncle Alex, may I present my wife, Princess Tiani Sayid.

"I am honored to meet you, Your Highness." Alex's words held a reverence unfound in previous introductions, the kind of reverence that comes with having known the royal family personally and holding them in high esteem.

Having heard this sentiment many times in the past few days, Tiani now had an appropriate answer. In broken English she said, "My honor also. No English. I speak Spanish."

Alex transitioned into Spanish and never missed a beat. There were so many members of the Sayid, Stephenson, and Cohen families who had one or more family members with language barriers that they had all become fluent in Spanish. Many also knew Arabic and Hebrew.

"Whose house is this?" Levi looked around at the forest and the sprawling home that seemed to be symbiotic with the trees and waterfall.

"This home belongs to Prince Marcos and his wife, Princess Hazel. They raised their boys here, and I was their unofficial leader."

"You are still our leader," a confident and handsome man said as he stepped out the front door. To his credit he was already speaking Spanish. He was about the same age as Uncle Alex and joined them at the edge of the sidewalk. "Even though you were younger than all of us."

"Gus, this is my nephew, Levi, one of my cousin's twins. And this lovely bride of his is Princess Tiani Sayid. Princess, may I introduce your cousin, Prince Augustus Sayid of Madain Saleh."

Unlike all the other men who had met Tiani, Gus didn't attempt to shake hands, nor did he bow his head respectfully to the princess. He boldly and confidently took Tiani in his arms and hugged her. "Welcome to our family."

When he pulled back slightly, they held each other at arm's length, and both had tears glistening in their eyes. "Thank you," Tiani said. "I'm so glad to meet you. I wish my father could be here."

"Perhaps we can visit him someday," Gus said.

"I'm sure he would like that." Tiani nodded, wiping her cheeks. "We didn't realize we had any other family until we met Levi and his brother."

"Our father should tell you more about what he knew of you," Gus said. "Come inside. I'll introduce you."

"How many people are here?" Levi asked as they made their way up to the ornately carved front door, worried about overwhelming Tiani.

"Just our wives, and the prince and princess," Gus replied. Levi must have looked confused because Gus added clarification. "My father and mother."

"Oh, right. That makes sense." Sort of. With all the royal family around, Levi wondered why Gus seemed to refer to his parents and *the* prince and princess.

"Later, others in our family will trickle in and out," Gus said, holding open the door to the elaborate home. "We can be a rowdy bunch when we all get together. We didn't want to overwhelm you."

"We appreciate that, thank you," Levi said, giving his wife's shoulders a little squeeze. Together they entered the infamous tree house, not sure what to expect.

Chapter Forty-Nine

He Misses You Too

Tiani's eyes were wide with wonder at this unique structure that seemed more tree than house. The main floor was one large open space with kitchen, dining, and living room seamlessly connected.

"How large is this home?" Levi asked, marveling at the wall of full-length windows that opened up to include the outer patios as additional living space. From what he could see from the angle of the foyer, the house and patio seemed to hang over the waterfall with barely a railing separating them from a sheer drop.

"We have six bedrooms, four stories, two guest houses, and a studio, all connected with a series of covered walkways."

Levi glanced up at the ceiling, confused. If he remembered correctly from what little he'd seen walking in, there was only a second story above the main level. Gus smiled.

"The other two stories are below us and follow the line of the waterfall so that almost every room in the house has a view of the water," Gus said.

"Wow." Levi could hardly picture the setup, and he was standing right here. He understood why they said he'd have to see the treehouse to understand. The architect should have won an award for this design, and probably had.

A man and woman who looked to be Levi's grandparents' age rose from the patio furniture overlooking the waterfall and stepped back into the house through the wall of windows. Although both had a regal air, they seemed down-to-earth and friendly. Levi had no doubt he was about to be introduced to Prince Marcos and Princess Hazel.

Sure enough, Gus introduced Levi and Tiani to his parents and then held out his arm as if displaying his cousin. "Mother, Father, this is Princess

Tiani Sayid." They must have picked up on the cue that Spanish was the preferred language because they started the conversation in Spanish without hesitation.

"My dear, welcome to our family." Princess Hazel drew Tiani close and held her for a long moment before releasing her with the same glistening eyes as that of her son Gus. "We're so glad to meet you."

Tiani, too choked up to even answer, just nodded and allowed herself to be pulled into the arms of Prince Marcos. He closed his eyes and held her as if she was a long-lost sister he'd never met. Pulling away, he whispered with emotion, "Tell me your lineage." The excitement in Marcos's voice was encouraging.

With practiced elegance, Tiani stated, "I am the daughter of Chief Gabor Sayid, granddaughter of Eadrich Sayid, great-granddaughter of Emir Sayid, great-great granddaughter of Prince Marcos Sayid."

"After Prince Marcos passed away, his son, Benjamin, my father, told me that he had a brother, Emir, who he had never met. Naturally, I was shocked because I thought my father was an only child."

"Why had they never met?" Tiani asked. Without any invitation or request, Tiani and Prince Marcos lowered to sit on the sofa, and they turned halfway so that they faced one another.

"My parents raised me mostly in the United States, but I traveled back and forth to Mexico several times a year. Sometime after my grandmother, Princess Lyla, passed away, grandfather met Akna and fell in love. My father didn't live in Mexico full time until after grandfather became ill. By then, he was too sick to visit his wife and Emir. I don't know much else."

"What about your father?" Levi asked, lowering to the sofa beside his wife. "Where is he now? Is he still alive?"

"He is." Marcos smiled at Levi. "My father lives just south of Cancun in a little town called Puerto Aventuras."

Levi turned to Tiani. "Maybe we could go visit Prince Benjamin when we go home to Guatemala. He could probably tell us more about Prince Marcos."

"By the way, you can call me Mark, rather than Marcos. Most people do."

"Mark," Tiani said, trying out the name. "My cousin."

"Yes, your cousin." Mark squeezed Tiani's hands and then glanced up at Levi. "Thank you for bringing her here to meet us."

"Your son, Gus, is friends with my uncle, right?" Levi glanced outside to where Gus and Alex sat on the porch with their wives, Phoebe and Ellen.

"Yes, but the relationships go back much further than that," Mark said. "His father is my advisor."

"Advisor? Like, financial advisor?"

"No." Mark chuckled. "Like... my *royal* advisor."

"I don't understand."

"He was designated as such during my coronation, and that was a lifetime assignment of service," Mark explained. "He has taken a vow to stand by my side as my brother, almost closer than a brother, really, second only to our wives. He is the keeper of my crown. My eyes and ears whenever we are called upon to serve. If I should be asked to serve as king, he will return to Madain Saleh with me."

"I thought Madain Saleh no longer existed." Levi's brow furrowed, confusion warring with everything he thought he knew about the royal family.

"Madain Saleh is no longer a nation state, nor do we hold a seat on the United Nations Security Council," Mark said. "But as long as there is still a member of the Sayid royal family willing to sit on the throne, the Saudi's tolerate us." Mark chuckled.

"Who is the king now?" Levi asked.

"Another one of our cousins." Mark stopped when the door opened and another couple entered the foyer. Mark patted Tiani's knee. "A story for another time, perhaps. I want you to meet my son, Hayden, and his wife Miranda, daughter of our reigning king. You'll have to ask her about that sometime." Mark stood and smiled at his son and daughter-in-law. The next person to arrive was the third of the brothers, Prince Owen, who had never married.

Levi and Tiani stood, and she tucked herself close. The room was getting crowded, and the ever-present rush of noise from the waterfall raked an added measure of stress to Levi's nerves. He could imagine how Tiani must be feeling. He gave her shoulders a little squeeze and whispered down to her. "You doing okay?"

"I'll never keep track of all these names," she whispered back.

"That's okay, they won't expect you to." Levi kissed the top of her head and kept his arm around her.

Alexander, Sr., and his wife, Krystina, arrived next, and Levi evaluated the relationship between him and the prince.

Although he'd never known about the royal advisor arrangement, he could see the connection immediately now that it had been pointed out.

Mark and his advisor reminded Levi of how close he and his twin were. A pang of longing pulled at Levi's heart, and he had a sudden desire to call Nicholas. Maybe after Prince Aaron and his wife arrived.

He didn't have to wait long. Prince Aaron strode in with a surprise, to Levi and Tiani anyway. No one had thought to mention that Aaron's wife, Felicia, was from Guatemala and even knew a few words in Yucatec. Not very many, but Felicia and Tiani connected in a way none of the others had. Felicia's Spanish even had a similar Guatemalan accent. For the rest of the evening, the two women were inseparable.

Levi was glad Tiani had found a kindred friend among the group. This allowed him the freedom to converse more freely with his uncle and get to know the other princes. He also remembered that he planned to call his brother.

He got Nicholas on a video chat and held up the phone to the room and called out, "Everyone say hello to Nicholas and his wife, Becky!"

There was general mayhem as the group called out hellos, then Levi brought the phone around the room to introduce each person. Nicholas was excited to see his Uncle Alex, but they knew they would see each other in two weeks for the wedding. Felicia told Nicholas and Levi that her father was their grandfather's cousin. Then Hazel interjected that Felicia's father was her cousin also, since she and Alex were cousins.

"There are too many cousins," Tiani said, and everyone laughed with her. That was an understatement.

Eventually Levi stepped away from the rest of the group and had his brother alone on the video chat. He looked out the kitchen window over the majestic waterfall and tried to hold the phone in a way that Nicholas could see.

"You'll just have to come here sometime to see for yourself," Levi said. He felt a catch in his throat and switched to English since it was just the two of them. "I miss you, man."

"Don't you dare start crying, Levi Stephenson," Nicholas said, but Levi could tell Nicholas was fighting to maintain composure also. "We're gonna see each other in just a couple of days."

"I don't know if I can do this, Nick." He hadn't called him by his nickname in years. "Tiani's homesick. I'm homesick. We love being married, but this sucks. I need you."

"I know." Nicholas said. "I know. I know. I know." Now they were both crying and neither of them could even speak.

Levi ducked out the front door and escaped to the privacy of his car, not wanting all those poised members of the royal family to see him break down. He laid his head against the steering wheel and sobbed, neither of them speaking. "I need you to come home."

"I can't, Lee. I'm planning a wedding. If I leave, Becky will kill me. You come here. Bring Tiani and come here to Houston. You can go see her family after the wedding, but at least you and I can be together."

"Okay," Levi choked out. "We'll come there. We'll leave in a couple days."

"If you have to, you can fly," Nicholas said. "I can get the dang car later. Don't worry about that."

"We'll be okay driving." Levi pulled himself together. "Knowing how soon I'm gonna see you will help."

Suddenly the passenger side door opened and Tiani slipped into the front seat. She bypassed Spanish and transitioned right into Yucatec. "Levi, are you okay?"

"Yeah, I just miss my brother," Levi answered, also in Yucatec. She leaned closer and wrapped her arms around his neck.

"Hi, Tiani," Nicholas called out through the video chat. They all transitioned right back into Spanish.

Tiani waved to her brother-in-law, all three of them wiping tears from their cheeks.

"Tiani, will you do me a favor?" Nicholas asked. When she nodded, he continued. "Will you bring that husband of yours over here to visit his twin brother? I miss him really bad."

"He misses you too," she said. "Yes, I'll bring him to you."

"Do you want to fly?" Nicholas asked. "Or drive my car?"

"I don't want to fly ever again," Tiani said, and both boys laughed with her. They all knew the only way she was going to go home to her family was to be brave and get back on a plane. "We will drive. Your car is fast."

"Yes, it is." Nicholas nodded. "How do you like America?"

"In America I am a princess. In my village I am just a tribal leader." They all laughed. It was good to have Tiani joking around. "I am learning English."

"What can you say to me in English?" Nicholas asked, in Spanish.

"I have learned to say, 'no English'."

"That is a very good phrase to learn," Nicholas said, laughing.

"She turned our dining room table into a study area," Levi said.

"So, in other words, it's just a typical day at our house," Nicholas said.

"Exactly."

"Well, hey, you guys better get back into that party," Nicholas said. "We'll talk in a day or two and make some plans."

"Thanks for chatting with me, man," Levi said. "Sure miss you."

"Anytime, little brother."

They ended the video chat, and Levi turned to Tiani and switched to Yucatec. "Thanks for coming to find me."

"That's what a wife is for." Tiani leaned forward, and they pressed their foreheads together, connecting for just a moment before going back inside.

Chapter Fifty

Good to Be Home

After one night at the tree house, and another night in Cambridge, Levi and Tiani closed up the townhouse, not knowing how many weeks or months they'd be gone.

Having reconnected in the car after crying together, they came to the understanding that they were both a little homesick and that was okay. They were better able to support each other with open communication.

Along the road from Cambridge to Houston, Levi chose the nicest high-end hotels he could find and requested the presidential suite or something close to it. What should have taken three days and two nights dragged out to four days of driving and three hotel rooms.

Tiani continued to love hot showers but had also discovered the luxury of Jacuzzi tubs. Levi wondered if spoiling her like this was a good idea. Once they returned to her village, she wouldn't have these amenities. Or flushing toilets. Or running water. Or electricity. Maybe spoiling her *was* a good idea. She'd be more open to the idea of returning to the States if she missed modern conveniences.

One of the things she desired most was something they *could* take back to the village, education. And that was one thing Levi was well-prepared to provide. He loved learning almost as much as she did, and he was a good teacher. They spent hours every day reading and learning. As they drove, Levi would read the road signs out loud in English and translate them in Yucatec or Spanish, explaining concepts she didn't understand.

By the time they arrived in Houston, Tiani had a basic fluency in spoken English and was quickly on her way to learning the written forms of English and Spanish.

Before checking into their hotel in Houston, Levi and Tiani drove straight to Nicholas and Becky's house in the University Oaks subdivision. A favorite among faculty members, the neighborhood sported homes nicer than the townhouse Nicholas and Levi shared in Cambridge and much larger. Becky's house even had a pool with a fenced-in yard. Children rode bicycles and couples walked dogs. A middle-aged man jogged past wearing earbuds and sweating through his T-shirt.

Pulling the Lamborghini into the driveway next door to a minivan on one side and a Volvo on the other was a little surreal. Levi opened the driver's side door and stood beside the car, then he removed his sunglasses and tossed them into the cupholder. Tiani had grown accustomed to letting herself out of the passenger side without waiting for Levi to come around and open the door for her, so she was already out of the car and stretching to shake out her stiff legs from the long drive.

The front door to the house opened, and before Levi could register that his brother had come outside, Nicholas had him in his arms and didn't let go. The twins stood there in the driveway for several minutes, just holding each other.

Somewhere at the periphery of his mind, Levi heard Becky welcome Tiani, and they hugged and talked for a moment before disappearing into the house. And still Levi couldn't let go of his brother.

They must have looked like a couple of geeks, standing there for that long, but Levi didn't care. They didn't talk. They didn't cry. They just clung to each other. Levi wasn't sure how long. Eventually his stomach growled from smelling the grill cooking burgers at a neighbor's house, and they both laughed, pulling back and looking each other up and down.

"I can breathe again," Nicholas said.

"How are we supposed to live apart?" Levi asked.

"I don't know if we can."

"We have to," Levi said. "You live in Houston now and I live... gosh, I don't even know where I live."

"You gonna keep teaching at Harvard?" Nicholas asked.

"I told Dr. Sedwick I'd be back for fall semester," Levi said. "Do you think this will get easier?"

"I don't know," Nicholas admitted. "We'll just take this a day at a time."

"Dr. Stephenson?" a man spoke from the sidewalk, the same man Levi and Tiani had seen jogging near the entrance to the subdivision.

"Yes?" both Levi and Nicholas answered, and the man did a double take.

"Uh... there are two of you." The man's eyes were wide as if he'd never seen identical twins before.

"That's what our mom said when we first popped out, and our lives have never been the same." They all chuckled at Levi's jest, and he stepped over to shake the man's hand. "I'm Levi, the smarter of the geek twins." Levi fought the urge to wipe his hand on his slacks. The guy was dripping in sweat.

"Nice to meet you. I'm Gary Peters. I teach in the biology department."

"Harvard," Levi said. "Linguistics."

"Just visiting your brother?" Gary asked. "We've enjoyed getting to know Dr. Benson's new husband these past two weeks. My wife and I live next door. She teaches elementary English."

"Have we really been apart for two weeks?" Nicholas asked, glancing at Levi with creased brows. "No wonder I'm feeling withdrawals."

"Two weeks too long," Levi mumbled, then turned to Gary. "We should introduce our wives. Yours teaches English, mine's *learning* English."

"Really? What's her native language?" Gary tilted his head.

"Yucatec," Levi said. He could tell from the confusion on Gary's face that he wasn't familiar. "Mayan."

"Oh, okay." Gary wiped his brow. "The real reason I interrupted your little hug fest was to ask about this incredible car. Is it really a... Lamborghini?"

"Yeah, Lamborghini Urus." Nicholas sighed, running his hand along the top of the car. "My brother brought my baby to me before he flies back to Guatemala after the wedding."

"Wedding? I thought he said he was already married," Gary said. "I'm confused."

"My wife and I are having a wedding for our families, since we eloped six weeks ago," Nicholas explained.

"That would explain why Dr. Benson left for the winter a single woman and came home with a husband." They all laughed. "Anyway, I need to get a shower. Let me know when you want to get our wives together." Gary pointed at Levi.

"And *you* let me know when I can take you for a drive," Nicholas said with a gleam in his eyes.

"I'll take you up on that, man." Gary pointed at Nicholas as he walked backward across their adjoining lawn.

"Nice neighbors," Levi said, patting his brother on the shoulder.

"Very nice." Nicholas reached into the car and popped the locks, then opened the trunk and lifted one of Levi's suitcases out. Handing the case to his twin, he said, "There's no way you're checking into a hotel tonight. I'm not letting you out of my sight until it's time for your plane to leave for Guatemala."

"You'll change your mind in a few hours when Tiani starts undressing me with her eyes."

"Shoot, she undresses you with her eyes all day long," Nicholas mumbled. "But you're right that I'll change my mind later tonight. I'll put your suitcases in the extra bedroom suite."

"Dang, it's good to be home," Levi said. Even though he'd never been to Houston before, he knew his twin understood the sentiment. Home was wherever they were together.

Chapter Fifty-One

Lovely Party

Over the next few days, people began to arrive in preparation for the wedding, including the twins' parents and grandparents, Uncle Alex and Aunt Ellen, Becky's parents, sisters, brothers, friends, aunts, uncles, and grandparents. They all stopped by the house, said hello, met Nicholas and Levi, along with Levi's new bride, then headed off to check into hotel rooms.

Levi's mom brought Tiani's dress from the dressmaker, and Becky was politely impressed but also noticeably envious. Levi had been right; Tiani's dress was going to upstage the bride. Oh well. Too late now.

Their mom had already spent an exorbitant amount of time with Tiani and focused her attention now on getting to know Becky. Although there was no language barrier, there was an obvious intelligence difference between the two.

It wasn't Becky's fault she was brilliant. Being surrounded by PhDs all day at work and in her neighborhood, Becky didn't have to try to dumb-down her conversations as she did with the twins' mom.

The bond that had formed between their mom and Tiani was recognizably more intimate, more like kindred spirits rather than in-laws.

As the wedding date approached, several things happened. Levi and Nicholas grew anxious because they knew they'd be apart again and didn't know for how long. Becky became a stressed-out bride and was overwhelmed with everything, and Tiani withdrew into her shell again.

Two days before the wedding, Levi decided it was time to take his bride and check themselves into their hotel room at the resort where the wedding would be held. He used the excuse that he wanted a little more privacy for late-night rendezvouses, but they all knew it was time to part ways.

Levi and Tiani did enjoy the in-room Jacuzzi tub and the additional level of privacy, but there was still an underlying tension to everything surrounding the wedding.

Tiani seemed reluctantly ready to go home, yet Levi wondered which home she was ready to return to, her new home in Cambridge with all its amenities, or the jungle in Guatemala where her family waited. He assumed she was homesick for her family.

The rehearsal dinner brought an additional unexpected wrinkle. Levi was expected to be Nicholas's best man, understandably, but he would be paired up with Becky's best friend, Simone. Tiani didn't understand what that meant and seemed genuinely confused when Levi held out his arm and Simone draped hers through his.

In Tiani's culture, no man would dare touch a woman who was not his wife. This betrayal went beyond jealousy. Simone was violating Tiani's husband.

Simone almost seemed smug about the pairing. Levi got the impression that she and the other bridesmaids were whispering behind Tiani's back.

Levi dealt with the brunt of Tiani's jealousy that evening in their hotel room, complete with a few choice words, several hours of the silent treatment, and sleeping on opposite sides of the king-sized bed they'd enjoyed thoroughly the previous evening. He knew the wedding day wasn't going to be any easier, but Levi hoped his doting on Tiani while introducing her to everyone would help.

Repeated introductions didn't help. At all. They'd been right that Tiani's dress upstaged the bride, and Levi's hasty departure from the wedding party immediately following pictures caused whispers. He'd been right that Becky's parents would see Tiani's dress as implying a double wedding. They didn't like that. This was a day for *their* princess, not Levi's. He didn't care. No matter whose wedding day this was, he would stand beside his wife.

Most guests at the wedding were oblivious to the tension within the bridal party and graciously met the beautiful and mysterious Mayan princess.

Her royal purple Magdalena satin ball gown was more formal than Becky's wedding dress. The style they had discussed, about braiding in feathers from her crown, turned out better than expected.

As the dinner ended and the dancing began, so did the excessive drinking. This, Levi predicted, was a disaster waiting to happen. Uncle Alex said goodnight very early in the evening, not willing to sit around and watch people indulge in the activity that put him in a coma for three days. Although the accident had happened over thirty years prior, the memory of lying in a hospital bed never really stopped haunting him.

Tensions finally came to a head when several very inebriated bridesmaids made fun of Tiani's broken English right in front of her, within earshot of several other people, including Levi and the bride and groom.

Tiani turned to Levi and asked in Yucatec what they said and why. When the girls laughed at the guttural sounding language of the Mayans, multiple people gasped.

"Excuse me, ladies," Levi interrupted them. "Her Highness was asking me to translate for her since she gave you the benefit of doubt, assuming you would never speak to anyone in such a condescending way."

"Her *Highness?*" one of the girls asked with a drunk giggle. "What is she? A queen?"

"I'm sorry, have I failed to introduce my wife?" Levi said through clenched teeth, attempting to maintain some level of civility. "May I present Princess Tiani Sayid, daughter of Chief Gabor Sayid, granddaughter of Eadrich Sayid, great-granddaughter of Emir Sayid, and great-great-granddaughter to the Crown Prince, Marcos Sayid of Mada'in Saleh."

"Huh?" the one girl asked, more confused than humbled.

Levi stepped a little closer. "I'll tell you what, when you can speak three languages, have lived on two continents, and are the daughter of a prince, feel free to criticize others for their *broken* English. Seeing as how the princess started learning English *last week*, she's catching on pretty quickly. Until then, learn some respect."

Levi turned to his wife and wrapped his arm around her shoulders to lead her from the room. Before leaving, he turned to his twin and Becky's family.

"Lovely party," Levi said. "Thank you for inviting us, but we're a little tired."

"Levi, wait—" Nicholas tried to stop him.

"Nicholas, please let go of my arm. I'll see you in the morning, before we leave for Guatemala."

Nicholas did as Levi requested, but the hurt in his eyes was something Levi had never seen before. He was reminded of his thought from a few days prior when he realized he would choose—and had chosen—Tiani over his twin.

The full extent of that realization hit Levi in the gut like a punch, and he felt nauseated. He couldn't leave the ballroom fast enough.

Chapter Fifty-Two

Through the Eyes of a Brown-skinned Woman

"**I** want to go home," Tiani said in perfect English, then switched to Yucatec. "Was that clear enough, or should I repeat it in Spanish for clarification?" She was storming down the hallway of the hotel as quickly as her high-heeled shoes would let her walk. She punched the button for the elevator to take them to the penthouse suites on the top floor.

"Tiani, I'm sorry they treated you that way." Levi stuck with Yucatec as he climbed into the elevator beside her. "That was uncalled for."

"I don't like America, and America doesn't like me." She folded her arms across her chest and huffed as the elevator soared to the upper levels of the hotel.

"That's not true," Levi argued. "Most people in America have been very kind to you."

"You don't see the way people look at me." Tiani stalked forward and poked Levi in the chest. "You see the world through the eyes of a white man. You do not know what it's like to be a brown-skinned person, especially a woman."

"You're right," Levi whispered, deflated. "I have never seen the world through the eyes of a brown-skinned woman."

Tiani lifted her chin and waited, probably expecting him to argue.

"But I have looked deep into the eyes of the most beautiful brown-skinned woman in the world, and I love what I see." Levi reached up and brushed the backs of his fingers along Tiani's cheek, and she leaned into his hand. He used the leverage to pull her gently to his chest so that her head was nearly on his shoulder.

"I don't belong in your world, Levi."

"You *are* my world, Tiani."

"I understand now why Akna didn't want to join Marcos in his world, and why Marcos couldn't stay in hers," Tiani said. "The Mayans and the white men were not meant to live together."

"Prince Marcos was hardly a white man. Middle Eastern men have very different skin tone than those of us from European descent."

"You're missing my point," she said, pulling back to look him in the eye. "You and I do not belong together."

"That's not true." Levi felt his world crashing down around him even as the elevator slowed and released them from their confinement.

There were only a few suites on the top level, and they were all occupied by members of his family. One suite was empty and would be for another couple of hours until the party downstairs finally died down.

Levi was glad he and Tiani had chosen a solemn ceremony with the tribe rather than a pretentious gathering of people they barely knew.

They let themselves into their suite, with Tiani still not speaking to Levi and he having no idea what to say to her.

Tiani marched into the bathroom and closed the door. The shower turned on, and Levi leaned his head against the doorframe, wishing he could join her but respecting her desire for solace. After just a moment the shower turned off, and Levi stepped away from the door seconds before Tiani opened the door and turned her back to him.

"I can't reach my zipper."

A tiny smile crept across Levi's face, seeing a perfect opportunity to connect with her. He took his time stepping closer and rested one hand on her hip and reached the other hand to lower her zipper slowly, savoring the clicking of the delicate tines. Before she could step away, he gently pulled the capped sleeves over her shoulders, letting the heavy dress fall away to reveal the creamy brown skin of her back.

Tiani gasped lightly as the shimmering violet fabric rested around her feet on the floor, and she stood there in feminine lacy underwear. Levi was reminded how unnecessary lingerie was because it would just wind up on the floor next to their bed.

He leaned forward and kissed her neck, running his hands up her arms. She shivered and leaned back against his chest, surrendering to his advance. He wanted to reassure her that they shouldn't allow the actions of a few mean girls to ruin their night, but he didn't want to distract her or remind her of the conversation from earlier.

They didn't need words. They didn't need broken English or accented Spanish or the exclusivity of Yucatec.

Levi would communicate with his wife using the best language in the world. Love.

Chapter Fifty-Three

Cutting the Cord

L evi was awakened by an insistent knocking on the door to his suite. He glanced at the bedside digital clock, which read 2:03 a.m. Only one person would be bold enough to bother him in the middle of the night.

He slipped on a pair of sweats and pulled the door to their bedroom closed to offer his sleeping wife a little privacy. He padded out to the suite's main door and opened it to find his twin brother, still wearing parts of his tux—the tie loosened and hanging around his neck, top button undone, cummerbund missing and jacket long abandoned.

"What?" Levi asked.

"I came to apologize," Nicholas said.

"At two in the morning?"

"This is the soonest I could get away." Nicholas pushed his way inside.

"Have you been drinking?" Levi asked. "You smell like a brewery."

"Dude, you know me better than that. Becky spilled a glass of beer, and it got all over my coat and some on my pants, and her dress was soaking wet."

"Where is your lovely bride?" Levi didn't even try to hide his sarcasm.

"Passed out in our suite," Nicholas grumbled.

"Some wedding night."

"Our wedding night was seven weeks ago," Nicholas said. "This was merely a party for her snobby friends and family."

"You married a winner," Levi said with a sneer.

"Becky's not like that. This is the first time I've ever seen her drink, which is probably why she got drunk so easily."

"Tiani has asked me to take her home from this wretched country where people are catty enough to treat others that way."

"They were drunk," Nicholas said. "They won't even remember what they said in the morning."

"Well, *my* wife remembers and will always remember and deserves to be treated better than that."

"I agree, and I'm sure Becky agrees. When she realizes what they said, she will feel terrible."

"I'm sure her hangover will be punishment enough." Levi stood. "Look, I'm going back to bed. We have a flight to catch in the morning, and you need to take care of your drunk bride. I'll see you in a few weeks or months or... sometime."

"Levi, don't do this," Nicholas said. "We're identical twins. A bond stronger than any other relationship in the world."

"No, Nicholas, our relationships with our wives are stronger than our relationships with each other. Now you need to go take care of your wife, and I need to take care of mine. This is the way life's meant to be. Time to cut the cord and go our separate ways."

"What if I don't want to go our separate ways?" Nicholas sounded as if he was going to cry. Levi needed to soften this goodbye.

"That's not a choice we get to make anymore." Levi pulled his brother into his arms, and they held each other. "Maybe sometime soon we'll live in the same town again, or at least the same country. But right now, we need to do what's best for our families. Your family is Becky, and my family is Tiani."

"I'll miss you," Nicholas said.

"I'll miss you too." Levi pulled back, and they looked each other in the eye, mirror images. "I'll have my satellite phone, and we'll call each other frequently. Plus, we still have 260 stelae to interpret. That's going to require us to stay in close contact. You may even need to come to Guatemala for an expedition. I can offer you a nice place to stay. We won't have running water or electricity, but we've got the best food this side of the equator."

They both chuckled, and Nicholas reached up to dry his eyes. Levi strode over to the door and held it open. Rip off the bandage.

"Goodnight, my brother," Levi said.

Nicholas met him at the door with one more hug. "I love you, Lee."

"I love you too, Nick."

They released each other from their hug, and Nicholas stepped out into the hall. Levi watched through the peephole as his twin hesitated by the door, then continued down the hall.

With his back against the door, Levi slid down onto the plush carpet of the finest suite of the resort and sobbed.

Chapter Fifty-Four

I Miss My Twin

The flight home to Guatemala was much less traumatic for Tiani than the flight north had been. She didn't need a sedative, and she enjoyed watching out the window at the clouds and the Gulf of Mexico far beneath. The main incentive to board the plane was her homesickness. Every mile brought her closer to her village and her family.

Levi never told Tiani about his late-night visit from Nicholas nor their tearful goodbye. He cried on the floor in their hotel suite until he had nothing left in him and then dragged himself to bed and crashed. In the morning, they packed up their things and left the hotel.

They brought more than they could reasonably carry through the four-hour trek from Tikal to the village, so they planned to have a truck arrive the following day and park near the edge of the jungle. Men from the village would meet them with empty backpacks and pick up the bundles, which were mostly books, and carry them back to the village.

The tribe members were beyond excited to welcome home their princess and her new husband.

Tiani and Levi had only been gone a few weeks, but so much had happened that those weeks felt like months.

An unwelcome surprise awaited them. The honeymoon cottage they'd stayed in after getting married was now occupied by another couple of newlyweds. There were no other available homes, which meant until they could build a house, Levi and Tiani were expected to live in her old bedroom in her father's home.

Levi wanted to hide his shock and disappointment, but his stomach clenched at the idea of sleeping a few feet away from his in-laws.

The bed was cozy, since there was barely room for the two of them to lay side by side. But the idea of sharing any intimacy was not appealing. Levi held Tiani in his arms, pushed up against the wall, sweltering in the humidity, and knew they couldn't sleep this way two nights in a row much less for months. He considered trekking back through the jungle the following morning and driving the hour down to Flores to check into a hotel.

"My tent!" Levi exclaimed in a whisper. "Tomorrow night we can move into my tent. Nicholas and Becky slept in their tent for five weeks after their wedding. It's got to be more comfortable than this."

"What?" Tiani turned over to grin at him. "You don't like sleeping in a cramped space with nothing but a thin wall between you and my father?"

"I miss our king-sized bed," Levi said.

"I miss our showers," Tiani answered with a provocative shift in her voice.

"I miss electricity," he said, only partially teasing.

"I miss air conditioning," she said, which was comical since she grew up without air conditioning.

"I miss my twin." The comment just popped out along with their rapid-fire list, but they both stilled at the realization. "I guess you've probably been missing your family as much as I'm missing my brother, huh?"

"No." Tiani shook her head. "I love my family, but there is nothing that compares to the bond between you and Nicholas. I've never seen anything like it."

"Really?" Why was this conversation making Levi feel hopeful?

"What's weird is that *I* miss Nicholas just from picking up on your loss."

"It's like a part of me is missing," they said almost simultaneously.

"We need to go home, Levi," Tiani said with resignation.

"We just arrived today." He was dumbfounded and confused.

"So, we'll stay for a few days or weeks and sleep in our tent, then insist that between now and when we return again my father build us a house."

"I would love that," Levi said.

"We could have a nice, big king-sized bed." Tiani snuggled close again with a suggestive tone to her voice.

"Don't even think about coming on to me because there is no way that's happening with your father listening."

"Darn." Tiani slumped into his arms. "We're putting up our tent tomorrow."

"First thing in the morning," Levi confirmed.

"Do you think it would be uncouth to take a nap after getting the tent set up?" Tiani asked.

"Probably," Levi admitted. "But I could feign a yawn a few hours later and use jet lag as a reason for fatigue."

"I like that plan," Tiani said.

"Let's get some rest now so we won't be too tired for any fun during naptime tomorrow."

"If you insist." Tiani turned around and tucked herself into his arms and, within minutes, was softly snoring.

Levi suspected he'd get zero sleep that night.

Chapter Fifty-Five

Unexpected Phone Call

T he tent worked well as a temporary solution, but Levi and Tiani agreed they wouldn't be staying in the village too much longer. They threw themselves into the task of teaching anyone who wanted to learn to read and write Spanish, and to speak English.

Levi loved watching Tiani read books to the kids of the tribe. They would sit around her, and she would try to sound out words. She knew Spanish well enough that, by using context clues, she was able to pick up reading rather quickly.

Tiani was very intelligent. He'd known that since their first conversation and from the way her eyes were always capturing her environment. But this was impressive.

He wanted to help her enroll in classes at Harvard when they returned home so she could dig deep into the languages. After the experience at the wedding reception when she'd been ridiculed for her broken English, she was determined to master the language.

Levi spent time each day over at the temple pyramid, often alone, studying the etchings and carvings, analyzing the collection. Some days he sat as far away as he could from the structure to look for any patterns not initially obvious. Other days he spent hours cleaning the stone carvings with a soft brush, evaluating them at the granular level.

In many ways, the weeks since he first stepped foot on this sacred site had been the best of his life. Most of what he was doing could be done from his climate-controlled office, but the *feel* of the temple site wasn't something that could be experienced through a computer screen.

The hypnotic peace of the afternoon was interrupted by a ringing and vibrating from inside his backpack, which sat on the ground near his feet.

He pulled out the satellite phone, expecting the phone number to be that of his brother or one of the other team members, but he didn't recognize the number.

He answered in English, hoping whoever was calling would be able to understand. "Hello, this is Dr. Stephenson."

"Levi, this is Mark Sayid, what are you up to?"

"I'm standing at the base of the most incredible temple pyramid ever created by the hands of men, interpreting ancient texts, and getting eaten alive by mosquitos the size of hummingbirds."

"Another day in paradise." Prince Marcos chuckled along with Levi. "How would you like to take a break and come meet my father?"

"Prince Benjamin? I would love that. Are you in Mexico?"

"Making preparations to head there in a few days. When my father learned who you had stumbled upon, he insisted I bring you and Tiani and her father to come meet him."

"Oh, what a great idea," Levi said, in awe. "Prince Benjamin. Wow. I never thought I'd have the opportunity. I'll return to the village and begin making plans. Shall we meet you in Puerto Aventuras?"

"That would be ideal," Prince Marcos said. "Do you need me to send you a private jet?"

"No, we bought one, but thank you."

"There's a resort there called the Barcelo Maya Palace. I'll book you a couple of suites, and you can arrive as soon as tomorrow, but I won't be there for at least another two or three days. I'll prepay for us to stay for several weeks. That way we can spend as much time as we'd like allowing all of you to get to know each other."

Levi was gathering his things together as they were talking, growing more and more excited. As he said goodbye to Prince Marcos, Levi turned to have one more look at the magnificent structure that had changed his life, not sure how soon he would return. Then he hurried into the tunnel to go find his wife and in-laws.

Time to introduce them to the modern world as well as connect them to their distant past.

Chapter Fifty-Six

Barcelo Maya Palace

Levi bit his tongue and reminded himself to breathe. This was Chief Gabor and his wife, Malayna's first time away from home. Although the chief had traveled to the nearby trading villages and rode in the Jeep down to Flores, he was uncomfortable about the four-hour flight to Cancun.

His wife, Malayna, had a very difficult time adapting. She'd never traveled outside the village even to shop at the trading villages. She got sick on the airplane; plastered her face to the window of the limousine, trying to see the Atlantic Ocean; was afraid to walk on the concrete sidewalks at the resort; and decided the bed in her suite was too soft before she even sat on it.

When Tiani tried to show her mother the running water from the sink in the bathroom, Malayna was terrified. They spent an inordinate amount of time explaining the indoor latrine, afraid Malayna would use the bushes beside the patio outside her suite.

After an afternoon of trauma, they ordered room service and sat together for a meal at the little table in Gabor and Malayna's suite, where Gabor discovered television.

Tiani helped her mother get ready for bed in her new and strange environment while Levi helped his new father-in-law learn how to use the remote control, a difficult feat even for people who had grown up with modern technology. Thankfully, some of the stations were Spanish language or this would have been a short trip back to the village.

When Levi and Tiani were satisfied that her parents weren't going to pee in the bushes or burn down the hotel, they said goodnight and snuck next door to their own suite.

They'd barely gotten the deadbolts in place before Tiani was dragging Levi toward her favorite modern amenity, the shower.

If anything in the world convinced Tiani to move back to civilization, it would be the shower. She loved standing under the cascading water and breathing the moist, steamy air even before she discovered how much fun they could have taking a shower together.

The king-sized bed was also a dream come true. Sleeping on the ground in the middle of a jungle for weeks was better than being crammed into a small bed with a thin wall between them and her parents, but having enjoyed the spacious townhouse in Cambridge, they knew what they were missing. And this was it.

Lying in each other's arms, soaking wet and not even caring that they'd likely need to request new bedding, Tiani smiled up at Levi from the crook of his arm, and he leaned down to kiss the tip of her nose.

"Don't make me go back to the jungle," Tiani teased. "I want to sleep in a bed with you every night for the rest of eternity."

"We can sleep anywhere you want, as long as you are by my side," Levi said.

"Admit it. That was way more fun than the jungle floor." Tiani reached over and tickled Levi playfully.

"You want to do it on the floor?" Levi teased right back, pulling her and the blankets to the edge of the bed. "If you insist."

"Don't you dare," she squealed.

"Oh, I dare," he said, rolling off the side, being careful to make sure he landed first to break her fall. With as many downy blankets and pillows that followed along with them, it wouldn't have mattered.

"You brat!" She hit him playfully, and he could tell she wasn't really angry.

"This plush carpeting is softer than anything we've slept on in weeks anyway." He rolled over so that he was looking down at her, and he brushed the strings of hair away from her face, grateful she'd thought to bring her cacao butter and combs along on their trip. For a moment they just stared at each other with soft grins. "You're so beautiful. How did I get so lucky to have you choose me for your husband?"

"My father chooses who I can marry," she teased. "I had no choice, remember?"

"Oh, you had a choice. You chose to place your hands on my chest, knowing that action would set into motion your carefully planned lure to get me to the altar."

"I couldn't help it." She whispered as she placed her hands on his chest once again. "I didn't plan that, or choose that, I just couldn't help it."

"Fate brought us together," Levi whispered back.

"I'm still sleeping up on the bed tonight," she said with a playful gleam in her eye.

"Not quite time to go to sleep though, is it?"

"Definitely not." Tiani wrapped her arms around Levi's neck and pulled him down for another long kiss.

Chapter Fifty-Seven

Pillow Fight

The sun was high in the sky by the time Levi was awakened by an insistent knocking on the door of their suite. Groggy, he dragged himself from the bed and pulled on the khaki shorts that were near the bathroom door where they'd been hastily discarded.

Not considering the intrusion could be anyone other than his wife's parents, and not awake enough to be embarrassed of the mess they'd created, Levi pulled open the door expecting to see his in-laws.

"Surprise," Nicholas said, standing in the doorway to their open suite with Becky by his side.

"What are you doing in Mexico?" Levi excitedly pulled his twin into his arms, then reached over to hug Becky.

"A certain prince gave us the heads-up that you two would be returning to civilization briefly, and we couldn't pass up the opportunity to come see you."

"I'm so glad you did," Levi said, stepping back for them to come inside.

Tiani sat up in bed, pulling sheets and blankets up to her chest, and rubbed her eyes.

Becky squealed and ran over, climbed onto the bed, and hugged her sister-in-law, telling her how excited she was to see her and how terrible she felt about what happened at their wedding. Tiani chuckled nervously and patted Becky on the shoulder, not awake yet.

"What the heck happened in here?" Nicholas asked, picking up Levi's Polo shirt from off the floor and kicking Tiani's bra out of the way. There were more articles of clothing on the floor than there were in their suitcase.

"Gimme that." Levi pulled the shirt from Nicholas's hands and slipped it over his head.

"What'd you do, have a pillow fight?" Nicholas picked a pillow off the floor, along with one of many blankets strewn everywhere.

"Maybe..." Levi grinned over at Tiani, and she giggled. "It was nice to sleep on a bed again."

"If you slept on the bed, why are all your pillows and blankets on the floor?" Nicholas teased, picking up another blanket.

Levi shrugged, and Tiani giggled again. "We had a fun night. What can I say?"

"I can see that." Nicholas plopped onto the sofa and kicked up his feet, resting them on the low table in the middle of the room. "When are we going to brunch?"

"Don't you have your own suite of rooms somewhere in this hotel?" Levi asked.

"Right next door, actually," Nicholas said. "But it's way more fun pestering you."

"Pestering is a good way to describe it." Levi wandered around the room, gathering pillows and blankets and piling them back on the king-sized bed. "We need to get showered and dressed before we can go to brunch, so you need to go away for a little while."

"Come on, Nick," Becky said, clambering back off the bed. "Let's give them some privacy, and you and I can go next door and have our own pillow fight."

"I have never said no to a pillow fight." Nicholas stood from his spot on the couch and headed toward the door.

"I'm so glad you're here, man," Levi said. He gave Nicholas one more hug before shooing him from the room with the promise of going to brunch in about an hour.

Chapter Fifty-Eight

Sands of the Seashore

Levi led Tiani along the boardwalk and helped her down onto the powdery sands on the beaches of Puerto Aventuras.

"The ocean is as beautiful as you promised me it would be." Tiani's voice filled with wonder. A warm, salty breeze pulled at her skirt and teased her hair from its braid.

"I agree. But that's not why I brought you down here," Levi said. The Barcelo Maya Palace resort stood like a sentinel at their backs as they faced the Atlantic Ocean and the horizon beyond.

They walked forward but not close enough that the sand was wet from the encroaching tides. Levi needed the sand to be dry for this to work. He found just the right spot, then pulled Tiani's hand gently.

"Come sit with me," Levi said, lowering to a cross-legged position. She sat beside him, but he shifted so they were facing each other. "Do you remember when I told you how many people there were who belonged to your Mayan tribe?"

She nodded. "You said there were as many as the sands on the seashore, and I told you I didn't know what that meant."

Levi reached out and cradled her hand in his, then lifted a handful of sand and let it sift through his fingers and onto her palm. "This is sand."

Tiani pulled her hand closer to her face and observed the tiny pieces of silica.

"And this"—Levi drew his arm in a circle around them—"is the seashore."

"Oh, Levi." She gasped, her eyes wide with panic. "There is so much."

"That's how many of your people there were."

"Where did they all go?" she asked, a vulnerability to her words.

"We don't know." He shook his head sadly. "That's what we're trying to find out. And that's why we want to interpret the writings on the temple pyramid. Your family's story deserves to be told."

"What if we can't figure out what the story is about?"

Levi shrugged. "Then we're no closer to learning the truth than we were yesterday. But the advances in modern technology, just in the past few years, lead me to believe that we're going to figure it out."

"I want to know the story," Tiani said. "I want to know what they were trying to tell us with the writings they left behind."

"Me too." Levi felt emotion prick his eyes and heart.

"The more English I learn, the more I can help you translate," she said in Yucatec.

"I'll help you understand English, and you help me understand Mayan."

"You already know more about my people than I do." She pushed his shoulder playfully.

"Then I'll teach you that too."

"Will you take me back to your place of teaching?" Tiani asked. "I want to learn... everything."

"Yes, I'll bring you home to Cambridge and you can sit with me in my office and learn all you can from the good professors at Harvard University and we'll bring all that knowledge back to your people and teach them."

"After the rainy season is over," she said with a gleam in her eye.

"Yes, after the rainy season." Levi squeezed her hands.

"And after my father builds us a house." Her words were authoritative.

"Definitely." Levi leaned forward and kissed Tiani on her lips, then grinned. "But first, let's go meet Prince Benjamin." He helped her off the sand, and they brushed themselves off.

Before stepping onto the boardwalk to head back to the resort, Tiani crouched again and lifted a handful of sand. She let it sift through her fingers and glanced around one more time.

It was a lot to take in. Levi understood that. Now that Tiani knew, she was eager to learn the truth.

Chapter Fifty-Nine

Meeting Prince Benjamin

Prince Benjamin's mansion was located on the canal, with a view of the ocean and a boat slip to park a yacht, not that he owned one anymore. At 99 years old, he wasn't doing much traveling. Even so, he was still a spritely man full of energy and spunk. He even answered his own door when they knocked.

Levi watched in awe as Benjamin scanned the group of young people on his doorstep and immediately knew which girl was Tiani. He reached forward and gathered her close.

"Oh, mi pequeno," Benjamin said, pulling Tiani into his arms and calling her his little one. "Hija de mi hermano."

"Daughter of my brother," Levi whispered. Several times removed, but close enough.

"Hola, mi tio," Tiani returned the sentiment, calling him her uncle.

"Tell me all of your names!" Benjamin looked around at the group, with gleaming eyes and excitement on his face.

Levi stepped forward and wrapped his arm around Tiani's shoulders. "I'm Levi Stephenson and I'm Tiani's husband. This is my brother Nicholas and his wife Becky," Levi said, pointing to Nicholas and Becky with his other hand.

"Oh, twins!" Benjamin said, then glanced at his Prince Marcos and his wife, Hazel. "Just like our Hazel and her brother."

Levi wanted to correct him that identical twins were a little more rare than that, but he didn't. He'd forgotten that Benjamin's daughter-in-law was twin sister to Mateo, his father's best friend's son. Too many connections. He was dizzy trying to piece it all together.

Nicholas nodded to Benjamin and spoke up for the first time. "We are honored to meet you, Your Highness."

"Oh, the honor is all mine, my son!" Benjamin said. "What a treat this is!"

Levi decided it was time to introduce Prince Benjamin to the other important members of the Sayid family. He gently pushed his twin off to the side in order to bring forward Tiani's parents. "Your Highness, may I introduce your nephew, Chief Gabor Sayid and his wife Malayna."

Prince Benjamin inherently knew to switch back to Spanish as he stepped farther onto the porch and placed both hands on Gabor's cheeks, which suddenly had streams of tears. "Hijo de mi hermano." Son of my brother, just as he had named Tiani as his daughter.

Chief Gabor couldn't even speak through his tears, just wrapped his arms around Benjamin and laid his head on the old man's shoulder. They cried together for several long minutes as the rest of them held back to let them have this moment.

Others in the group also choked back tears, except Tiani, who tucked herself into Levi's arms and sobbed unabashedly, repeating over and over, thank you, thank you to Levi.

Over Tiani's shoulder, Levi caught Prince Marcos's attention and reached out to hold his hand. This was a big deal for Benjamin. He never knew his brother, and Gabor never knew that his great-uncle existed, much less was still alive. Even his great-great-grandfather was a mystery to him, but here was a chance to learn more about him.

When the two men finally pulled back from each other, Gabor looked into his uncle's face, with pure love combined with a childlike adoration. Levi had never seen such vulnerability in the strong, tattooed Mayan chief, who intimidated everyone in his presence.

"Come inside, my son, and sit with me awhile," Benjamin said in Spanish. "I will tell you all about your grandfather."

Continue reading the Royal Family Saga Book Four: Billionaire's Brother

Love Letter from Author Julie L. Spencer

O h, my friends, I love these characters. They are so special to me. I loved Levi's progression from this funny kid who teases his brother and has his nose in his books to a complete lovesick fool after he meets Tiani.

And I loved the vulnerability Tiani showed in going from this strong, confident woman to completely surrendering to this big, scary world she didn't know existed, and then back to this passionate, snarky, *Take me home. I don't like America and we don't belong together.*

I loved the way Nicholas changed after he started missing his twin. Kind of like how my eighteen-year-old daughter bawled the whole time she was packing to leave for her first big job in a different state far away when she'd been so confident and ready to go.

At the end of The Geek Twins, Prince Benjamin promises to tell his great-nephew the story of his great-grandfather. You might remember Benjamin's father from the first few chapters of Billionaire Crown Prince when Prince Marcos handed the title to his grandson, Mark and commanded that Mark and Hazel marry and have lots of beautiful babies.

For the next book in the series, travel back in time to when Prince Marcos Sayid ignored deathbed promises to his older brother, Crown Prince Jared Sayid; defied the king; married a woman he'd known for eight minutes; and escaped with their newborn son, Prince Benjamin, before his brother's widow could follow through with her threats against his family.

Two generations later, the fate of the Kingdom of Madain Saleh hangs in the balance trying to survive evil princesses, secret murder plots, and a contested crown. Conclusively discover the identity of the final king of

Madain Saleh. Grab your tissues before you begin the story of The Last Prince.

God bless you, my friends. Stay safe! *-Julie L. Spencer*

Billionaire's Brother

Continue reading the Royal Family Saga Book Four: Billionaire's Brother

Three love stories, One contested crown, and the final ruler of the Kingdom of Madain Saleh.

Prince Marcos Sayid claims the title of Crown Prince when his brother, Jared Sayid, dies suddenly in a motorcycle crash. Forced to marry immediately and produce an heir, Marcos proposes to Lyla Donovan, a girl he's known for eight minutes, and whisks her away on an exotic honeymoon only to come home to his kingdom on the brink of civil war. Not willing to risk the life of his young bride and their newborn prince, Marcos takes the crown and a few devoted subjects and flees the country.

Two generations later, with the fate of the kingdom hanging in the balance, Prince Elmer Sayid quietly leads from behind his domineering older brother. Having been told all his life that his bloodline is insignificant because he's so far removed for the title of Crown, he marries his childhood sweetheart, Savannah, even though she isn't a princess, nor does she hold a title. Yet, Elmer is the only prince left to hold the hand of the king when he takes his last breath.

With their kingdom brushed off the map like the sands in the Arabian Desert, Elmer and Savannah's son, Prince Ethan, takes their billions and their blessing, and escapes to America, determined to put their money to good use before he succumbs to his end-stage cancer. Ethan didn't count on falling in love with his estate planning attorney, Natalie Dolan, a few days before his body was ready to give up.

Will Ethan be the last prince of Madain Saleh?

Continue reading the Royal Family Saga Book Four: Billionaire's Brother

About Author Julie Spencer

Julie is a bestselling multi-genre author who writes under three pen names. Her young adult sports romance have a little less spice and little more sweet-n-innocent. As Julie Spencer and Julie L. Spencer, she writes books with more serious subjects and maybe some religion thrown in.

Her more controversial books can be found under the new pen name J.L. Spencer. These books come with a content warning and may contain a little more heat, spice, and perhaps a few discussions about or trips to the main characters' bedrooms.

All of her stories include snarky, flawed characters, and romantic twists and turns. Julie believes we can change the world one story at a time.

www.AuthorJulieSpencer.com

All's Fair in Love and Sports Series

Take Me to the Winter Games

Meet Me at the Summer Games

Ride the Halfpipe with Me

Pass Me the Ball

Catching Waves with You

Strike Three, You're Mine

Meet Me at Half Court

Cheer for Me

Basketballs and Mistletoe

Running to You

Matching You with Love
(with co-author Audi Lynn Anderson)

All's Fair in Love and Sports Collection

Prince of Israel Series on Kindle Vella

First Prince of Israel

(Prequel to the Prince of Israel Series)

Royal Family Saga Series

Billionaire Crown Prince

Billionaire Hero

Billionaire Professors (The Geek Twins)

Billionaire's Brother

Billionaire's Sons

Honorary Prince

Royal Family Saga Special Editions

Royal Family Saga Volume I

Royal Family Saga Volume II

Royal Family Saga Volume III

Love Letters Series

Who Wants to Marry a Mormon Girl?

Who Wants to Marry a Billionaire Gamer?

Christian Romance

The Cove

The Farmer's Daughter

The Man in the Yellow Jaguar

The Refusal

Rock Star Redemption Series

Almost a Rock Star

Billionaire Rock Star

International Rock Star

Fallen Rock Star

Forever a Rock Star

Rock Star Redemption Series – Complete Collection

Opening Act: Buxton Peak Meets Infusion Deep

Opening Act: Infusion Deep Meets Buxton Peak
(with co-author Lara Wynter)

Julie writes some more controversial books under the pen name J.L. Spencer

These books may contain heat, spice, and perhaps a few discussions about or trips to the main characters' bedrooms.

Here is a list if you'd like to check them out:

Road Trip

Combustion

A Million Bucks

Hidden Swan

She's Not My Sister

Nonfiction

Writing Romance Is Not About Sex... or Is It? How Far Is Too Far in Clean Romance?

How to Outline a Romance Novel – Fiction Writing Skills for Romance Authors

How to Write a Romantic Subplot – How to Add Romance to Other Plot Structures

Listen to audiobooks by Julie L. Spencer

All's Fair in Love and Sports Series

<u>Running to You</u>

<u>Meet Me at Half Court</u>

<u>Pass Me the Ball</u>

<u>Basketballs and Mistletoe</u>

<u>Strike Three, You're Mine</u>

Social Issues

<u>Combustion</u>

Royal Family Saga

<u>Billionaire Crown Prince</u>

Billionaire Hero

Love Letters Series

Who Wants to Marry a Mormon Girl?

Who Wants to Marry a Billionaire Gamer?

Rock Star Redemption Series

Almost a Rock Star

Billionaire Rock Star

International Rock Star

Fallen Rock Star

Forever a Rock Star

Rock Star Redemption Series Complete Collection

Christian Romance

<u>The Cove</u>

<u>The Man in the Yellow Jaguar</u>